To Be

The Giant Slayer

Thank you for contributing to making this a reality!

[illegible]

The Giant Slayer

First Kings | Book One

N.A. HART

WRITTEN DEER PUBLICATIONS
GRAND RAPIDS

For Will,

I started writing this just for you, but I hope you don't mind that I've shared it with the world.

Contents

Lexile Measure: 730L

Cover design: *Jessica Bell*

Back cover copy: *Mary Loebig Giles*

ISBN: 978-0-9965745-1-8

Library of Congress Control Number: 2015913607

Visit http://writtendeer.com

1. Bethlehem. Late summer, 1028 bce

David carried himself as stiff and straight as a dried stalk of white squill—at least until he was out of Father's sight, when he kicked first one stone, then another, and then ran all over the path like a crazed goat, attacking every pebble larger than his thumb pad. All his brothers had gotten to spend their twelfth year at Father's side. This was supposed to be *his* year.

The trip to Uncle Jonathan's took twice as long as usual.

Once there, he searched around and found his uncle on his haunches, repairing a section of wall.

His mother's brother looked up and grinned. He pushed himself upright and David endured the usual kiss on each cheek. "I was glad to hear that Jesse is finally looking into expanding his flocks. This way we get to spend...."

David glanced up when his uncle paused.

"You're not as pleased as I am, I take it?"

Uncle Jonathan's kind smile wasn't helping. David had to look away and grit his teeth.

"I see." Uncle Jonathan crouched back down and pointed at a low section of the wall. "I'm filling in this hole where some creature managed to dig under the stones."

David knelt beside him and peered at the hole, because that was clearly what his uncle expected.

"I like to mix thorns in with the mud. Make it less pleasant for whatever dug this in the first place." Uncle Jonathan pointed at a pile of thornbush several paces away. "Your first job is to break off the thorns, and then gather them and put them in this slurry. Use the fat end of my staff and your feet." He turned back to the wall.

Was that really necessary? Or was it just his uncle's way of letting him work out his anger? That was David's mother's method, and with eight boys, someone was always losing his temper. He dragged the staff to the pile.

"Tamp it down a bit before you go at it," Uncle Jonathan called.

David held the staff upright and used the knot end to compact the tangled branches. When that didn't work, he stomped on the pile and a thorn got him in the ankle. He was twelve now, so he tried not to yell, but the thorn had gone in all the way. Blood ran down his foot.

"Looks ready," Uncle Jonathan yelled.

David wiped his foot against the hem of his tunic, stepped back, swung the staff over his head, and brought the knot down, hard. Over and over and over. Each time he made contact with the ground, his arms shuddered. With every swing, something his father said to him rose up like bile.

"You're the youngest of eight sons. Stop acting like you'll ever have anything of your own."

He'd only asked for two lambs so he could experiment with some methods he'd heard about from other shepherds. He hadn't meant Father to think he was planning to go off with a herd of his own.

"Stop trying to prove that you're better than your brothers. After I'm gone, you'll be in one of their households."

He wouldn't join Eliab's household. He wouldn't!

"If you don't stop showing off, I wouldn't blame them for pulling a Joseph on you and selling you to slave traders."

Sweat clouded his vision until he wasn't sure he was hitting the thornbush anymore, but he kept bashing away.

"That's enough."

David whirled around and it all came billowing out: how he didn't expect any kind of feast, but all his brothers got to start their training with their father on their twelfth birthday, and how nobody, not even his mother, had mentioned his birthday until the next new moon.

It was shameful to criticize his father like this, so he couldn't look at his uncle, but he couldn't stop his complaints, either. And then he felt worse because Jonathan was his favorite uncle, and here he was, resenting spending time with him. Tears and snot mixed with the grit on his skin every time he ran his forearm over his face. "The twelfth year is supposed to be a blessing from father to son. And what did I get?"

"Hold on, there." Uncle Jonathan held his hands up, palms out, as if David were a wild-eyed donkey.

David stared at the ground. If he looked up, would his uncle be pitying or disapproving? He didn't want to risk seeing either one.

"I'm going to tell you this once." Uncle Jonathan's voice was just above a whisper, so David had to shuffle closer to hear. "If you speak one word of it to Jesse, I'll deny it. But he is wrong. You do not lord it over your brothers. You do not show off for the village."

Finally, someone saw David's situation like he did.

"The Lord has blessed you. Nobody should deny that."

David squeezed his eyes shut. He'd cried enough already.

"But Jesse is also right."

"What?" David's eyes flew open.

Uncle Jonathan shrugged. "You *are* an eighth son. When Jesse dies you will live in one of your brothers' households and all your work will be for someone else's glory. That is the way it has always been."

That his uncle was speaking the truth made it worse.

"Your father sending you to me is a sign that he notices and appreciates your value to the family." Uncle Jonathan took his staff and used the narrow end to hook the dethorned branches and toss them to the side. "Your brothers are such horrible shepherds."

That was true. It was also true that David loved being in the hills where he was free to sing as loudly and as often as he wanted. He even liked the animals. So why did it still feel like an insult?

Uncle Jonathan scooped the thorns into a pile and they worked together to mix the mud plaster and fill the hole in the wall. His uncle explained each step in the process and demonstrated it before letting David try his hand at it, as patient as Jesse was critical.

"So." Uncle Jonathan clapped his hands together and stood. "This year will be good, yes?"

David rose and nodded seriously, like a man would. Because that's what this year was about: becoming a man. If his own father turned his back on him, he should thank the Lord that someone was willing to take him on.

He *should*, but he couldn't quite do it.

*****

Spring, 1027 BCE

The hills were the one place David was supposed to be free from his older brother. Eliab always said he'd go to Sheol before he'd set foot there again. But here he was, in the middle of the day, with the second youngest, Ozem, yelling, "Where are you, baby cheeks?"

David almost wished they were rustlers. At least then he could fight back without getting in trouble.

It was never smart to keep Eliab waiting, so he tore down the hill, leaping over rocks and skidding on loose sand and gravel, his tunic flapping between his legs.

"Don't get your loincloth in a bunch," Eliab said.

David gulped for air. "What is it?"

Eliab ignored him and shoved Ozem toward the animals. "You remember them, don't you?"

Ozem jerked his shoulder away. "Don't have to rub it in." He snatched the thick, knotted end of David's staff.

David tightened his grip. "What's going on?"

"What's going on is there's a feast but Father stuck me with the flock." Ozem yanked the staff away and stalked up the hill. "Did you fat tails miss me? I didn't miss you!"

"Yelling makes them nervous," David called up.

Ozem made a rude gesture.

"There are lions."

"I know," Ozem said. "I heard all about it yesterday."

David scowled at his brother's back, but since he had no say over anything, he turned to Eliab. "There's a feast?"

Eliab nodded. "And for some reason, they want you." His long arm shot forward and he twisted the top of David's ear, pulling him along a few steps. "Come on."

When Eliab finally let go, David clenched his fists at his sides to keep from giving his brother the satisfaction of watching him rub his aching ear.

"Move it, baby cheeks," Eliab called over his shoulder. "I'm not missing anything because I had to play nursemaid to you."

David scrambled to catch up. "This isn't a designated day. What's the feast for?"

"Samuel's here."

"The prophet?"

"That's what I said."

David whistled. No prophet had ever stopped in Bethlehem before.

"Came in this morning. Scared Father and the elders half to death." Eliab snorted. "You should've seen them, wringing their hands, worrying like old women. My wife's father piled dirt on his head."

"Again?"

"You don't get to talk about him like that."

David flinched, but Eliab only used words this time. "Does he seem different from other men?" It took so long for Eliab to speak that David resigned himself to not getting an answer.

"Remember when Grandfather Obed would tell the old stories?"

Shivers ran across David's skin.

"Imagine that tenfold and you have an idea of Samuel's power."

"Were you scared?" David wished he could take those words back the second they left his mouth. Father was right; he needed to stop asking every question that came to his mind. Eliab's fist rose and David braced himself.

"I was proud." Eliab pounded his own chest twice. "Not every farmer's son in Judah gets the privilege of watching the voice of God slice into the neck of a heifer and drain the blood off. This is a great day for Bethlehem."

They walked on in silence. David had to run now and then to keep up. "I still don't get why I'm needed."

"I don't either."

"Gue–"

Eliab cut him off with a glare and walked past the well.

David stopped to wash himself, but Eliab grabbed him by the upper arm and hauled him away.

"But I need to–"

"I'll make sure you're purified, alright." Eliab's smile was mean. "Who knows what you've been touching out there by yourself all day. We need moving water. Burak Spring still has some runoff." He kept hold of David long enough that David knew he'd have a cuff of bruises around his arm. When they got there, Eliab tripped him, smushing his face into the wet grass. "Run the water over your hands three times and be quick about it. Samuel won't let anyone sit down and eat until you're there."

David hurried through the ritual and then scrubbed his wet hands over his face and arms. "What? Why?"

Eliab pulled David up by the neck of his tunic, which

tightened like a noose across his throat, making him cough.

"All I know is that Father called me in from the fields. Samuel took one look at me and asked about the rest of you. I had to stand there, in front of the elders and everyone else, while each stupid brother came and the prophet kept asking whether there were any more." He pushed David along. "Father almost forgot about you. Don't humiliate us more than we already are."

"Did he do that for any other family?"

Eliab made a growling noise in his throat, and David heeded the warning: no more questions.

This definitely topped the excitement of driving off that mountain lion yesterday. David had been summoned by the prophet who'd brought Israel and Judah back to good standing with the Lord. Everyone was waiting for him. Him. A youngest son.

A snippet he'd been working on in the hills came to him and he could finish the third line:

> We're only a little lower than angels,
> yet You crown us with glory and honor.

When they were within sight of the threshing floor at the edge of town, Eliab squared his shoulders and stuck out his chest. He dug his thumb between David's shoulder blades. "Make an effort."

But David barely heard him. The entire village was

there, sitting on the ground in small groups, staring at him as if he'd grown extra arms. Wisps of smoke still rose from the ashes on the altar and the scent of burned fat and boiling meat made him dizzy. His father stood and waved from under the big tamarisk tree. The stranger next to him must be the prophet.

It wasn't merely duty that drew David forward. From twenty paces away, he could sense the authority coming from Samuel, but it was more than that. The prophet didn't glance around to make sure people were watching him, or hold himself stiffly, or sneer to prove his superiority. He just...was.

David smiled.

Samuel smiled back. "Here you are."

Nobody had taught him how to address a prophet. A bow was always appropriate, but he bent all the way over, because a dip of the head didn't feel like enough. In the middle of David's bow, the prophet removed an ox horn from his belt. David straightened. "I've washed in the spring, my lord."

"Hush." Samuel raised the horn above David's head and tipped it.

It wasn't water; it was oil.

The oil was warm, and surprisingly heavy. It smelled like cinnamon and tree sap. David closed his eyes as something he couldn't explain seeped through him. It uncoiled from the top of his head, down through the center of his body to every finger, every toe, through every hair. He flexed his hands.

Samuel put his hand on David's head and mumbled.

David exhaled and opened his eyes. He tipped his head up and met Samuel's solemn gaze.

The village was buzzing. David could hear everyone asking each other, "What?" "Why?"

The prophet had to hear it, too, but he merely blinked down at David before tucking the horn in his belt, walking to the middle of the threshing floor, raising his hands to the heavens and chanting a blessing, turning slowly. After the "amen and amen," he clapped his hands together and declared, "Let's eat!"

Oil dripped from David's hair into his eyes, making tracks down his cheeks and splotches on his tunic. What was he supposed to do now? When a prophet anointed you with oil, could you wipe it off? Or would that cancel the blessing or whatever it was? Drops of oil flew from the tips of his hair when he gave an experimental shake. Could his mother get angry that he got oil on his tunic when it was a prophet's fault?

His father rose to greet him with open arms. "That's my boy! I always knew he'd find favor."

David could hardly swallow past the lump in his throat.

Even more astonishing, Jesse made a big show of holding David's shoulders and kissing each cheek. David was almost relieved when his father returned to his usual form, kicking Eliab and snapping at his sons. "Everyone's watching."

"What are we supposed to do?" Eliab muttered.

"Act pleased for your brother."

His brothers lined up in age order and took turns making appropriate congratulatory gestures and saying expected words with their full voices, but they shied away from him as if the anointing oil were on fire.

Then the village elders crowded too close, clapping his shoulders and squeezing his arms as if the anointing would rub off on them.

"What an honor for our village."

"A feast and an anointing. We are blessed."

The fringe from Elder Maacah's mantle tickled David's cheek when the puffed-up man dipped his head to David's father. "You are blessed today, Jesse."

"Settle down, settle down," Jesse said once the elders were gone. He pointed an accusing finger at David. "Let's enjoy the feast without being pestered by questions."

The back of David's neck burned, and not from the mid-day sun.

"I can see them building up," Jesse said. "And don't get full of yourself, either. This doesn't mean you've earned a choice cut."

"Yes, Father." Of all the questions swirling in David like a sand devil, whether he'd get a better piece of meat wasn't one of them. His legs prickled. He couldn't sit still.

Soon, he couldn't sit at all. He popped up before he'd gotten his portion.

Eliab hissed at him to sit down and stop showing off, but he dodged his brother's reach and kept moving.

Without planning on it, he found himself walking to Samuel. "Excuse me, my lord."

Samuel turned around and clucked at him. He took the cloth that covered the bread platter and sopped up the oil still pooled on David's hair. "Adonai himself will tell you when the time is right." He wiped David's face and neck more tenderly than his own mother ever had.

"Does this mean I'm a prophet? I mean, that I'll be a prophet when I'm grown?"

"No, son. Adonai will reveal all in His own timing." Samuel leaned close and spoke into David's ear. "Enjoy His spirit. Learn to recognize it." He tapped his fist on the center of David's chest. "Lodge it in your heart. You're going to need it." With that, he turned back to his plate.

Need it for what? To endure decades of tending the flocks? To survive Eliab? To go out and....

For once, his imagination failed him.

How long would it take? A few days? Until the new moon? Could Adonai keep him in suspense for a whole season?

2. Gibeah. One year later. Early summer 1026 bce

Saul slouched on what passed for his throne: a pile of skins draped over a barely glorified stone bench. He picked at the lone ruby in the crown that sat on his lap.

It wasn't much of a crown, but it was the only one he had, taken from the bounty of his first defeat of the Ammonites, back in the days when *He* was happy. If *He* had let Saul keep the bounty from King Agag, he wouldn't be stuck with Nahash's battle back-up; he'd have the most impressive solid gold, jewel-encrusted crown. Not thin gold hammered over copper and dotted with gems like this piece of second-rate metalwork.

He held it up and looked through the center. It wasn't even properly round. No wonder it dug into his right temple. Saul tossed it and watched it scuttle across the plastered center of the floor until it passed a group of people at the other end of the room.

Why were they in such a tight group with their heads all together? And so far away? And whispering?

He had chosen Saul. Out of all of Israel, *He* had made Saul their first king. When was that going to be enough?

People with honorable intentions did not huddle and

act furtive. How dare they come into his receiving room and plot against him? Where was the respect for their king? The reverence? The fear?

One of his armor bearers was in the group; he didn't even flinch when the crown clattered past him. What if someone had crept in and cut off Saul's head while they were gossiping? What if they were conspiring to make that happen?

"What are you doing?"

They broke apart and looked anywhere but at him.

Saul reached to his right and brought his spear closer to him. To make them sweat, he toyed with it.

"What are you doing?" He liked to talk in a too-quiet voice. It was more threatening than shouting.

They migrated as a group to his throne.

"Stop that or I'll give you something to cry about."

Abner stepped out and bowed. "Our apologies, my lord. We didn't mean any disrespect." He straightened and pushed forward a youth whose beard was yet very short. "Your servant, Ba–"

"I don't care what his name is," Saul said.

"He's been working as your–"

"Why are you bothering me with details?" Saul leapt to his feet with his spear still in hand and loomed over the young man. "State your business and be done." He plunked back down. "I don't have time for this."

The servant ducked his head and apologized.

"Now."

The servant opened his mouth and no sound came out until Abner slugged his shoulder. "In Bethlehem, where I'm from, we have this boy. He doesn't look like much next to his brothers, but–"

Abner nudged him again.

"My lord, I know who can soothe you."

Saul lifted one eyebrow. "Who says I need soothing?"

"Forgive me, my lord, I didn't mean to imply that you needed anything, it was, I mean, I was told–"

Abner shushed him and got down on one knee.

This must be serious.

"Permit me, your humble servant, to speak freely."

Saul dug his thumbnail into the spear shaft. "You are not humble and you are not my servant, you're my cousin. Get up."

He didn't.

"Now." Saul banged the wooden end on the ground.

Abner looked pointedly at the spear, his face clearly communicating the thought, "Are you serious?"

It *was* pointless to try to intimidate the head of his army with a show of strength. Saul was taller, but Abner was wider and he trained more. Saul wasn't about to kill his general, and everyone there knew it, so he handed the spear to his idiot armor bearer and waved his cousin close enough for a private conversation.

"You're not yourself, lately," Abner said.

Saul would describe his state more forcefully: he was tormented day and night.

"You don't sleep. You kick over your food. Your women don't please you. This servant is convinced he knows someone who can help." Abner spread his arms in a wide shrug. "What does it hurt to hear him out?"

When Saul didn't reply, Abner leaned closer. "They're saying it's an evil spirit."

Saul clenched his fists until his knuckles were white. He'd been found out. He took a deep breath to give them the impression that he was calm and nodded at the servant to continue.

"In my village, there's a young man–"

"How young?"

The servant squinted. "Thirteen or fourteen."

"What position in the family?"

"Youngest of eight sons."

Saul smirked. "So the father will be happy to palm him off on someone else."

A few people in the room gave him a pity laugh, but the servant shook his head earnestly. "No. He cares for his father's flock."

His flock? "You think a shepherd is what I need?"

"Yes, my lord."

"A shepherd."

Abner hurried to whisper to the servant.

"Not, not his shepherding, my lord. He plays the lyre and sings."

A musician. All this buildup for a lousy musician? Not a witch or a healer who knew of some rare herbs nobody had tried yet? "A singing shepherd?"

The servant's face was transformed. "My lord, when he sings, you forget all your troubles. Every new moon feast, he sings songs of praise that get the old men leaping up and raising their hands. His songs of lament get everyone weeping."

"How?" Saul leaned farther back on his throne and slit his eyes at the servant. "Beautiful voice?"

"Yes." But he made it sound like that wasn't quite it.

"Skillful playing?"

"Certainly."

Saul was losing patience. He surged forward. "I have that already. By the dozens. Tell me you haven't wasted my time. Tell me this Bethlehemite has something else."

The servant bowed his head and whispered. "The Lord."

Saul put his hand behind his ear.

Abner prodded the servant, who flushed deep red and spoke up. "The Lord is with him. I can't explain how I know, but it's so clear..."

The servant kept babbling, but Saul no longer heard him.

The Lord.

It was all *His* fault. *He* had deserted Saul. *His* absence was causing all Saul's problems. If *He* was with this boy from Bethlehem, Saul might have a chance.

Saul made a show of seeming casual. "Fine. We'll see what he has."

"Thank you, my lord. Thank you." The servant bowed a half dozen times. "You won't regret it. He's brave and strong and will serve the king well."

"If the singing doesn't work out, we can always put him in the army." Saul smirked and anticipated the laughter he'd get, but everyone nodded. "That was a joke. Israel is not so desperate as to put boys on the battlefield."

The next day, long after the midday meal, Saul stood by a window in the receiving room watching an eagle ride the winds high in the sky, half-listening to his livestock manager going on about the oxen, when he became aware that the receiving room was silent. There were dozens of people there, none of them making a sound. He narrowed his eyes and did a slow scan.

Everyone was watching Abner lead a boy through the room. His tunic was of the plainest brown wool, stained, rough, and threadbare in spots, as if it had been handed down through many sons. He did not act like a servant, and he definitely did not look like a tribal visitor, but Abner was leading him.

And then it dawned on him: the boy was the singing shepherd.

Saul's eyes narrowed further. That's why the room was crushed with advisers and hangers-on. The entire city must be talking about him, gossiping about the king's problems. After avoiding him for days, now they crowded near to see whether this scheme would work. Meddlesome fools.

When the shepherd was within several steps of Saul, he dropped to his knees and bowed so low that his forehead touched the floor. "It's an honor to be called by Adonai's Anointed."

At least the boy was raised well. He knew how to pay the proper respect. "Who is your father?"

The shepherd stayed on his knees, but he straightened his upper body. "Jesse." His head remained bowed. "Of Obed, of Boaz."

"You say that as if it meant something to me." Saul strolled closer and rapped him on the top of the head with his knuckle. He played to the crowd. "Sons of the tribe of Judah are always such show-offs." To the boy, he offered a terse, "Get up."

Saul strode over to his throne and lowered himself with a flourish of his cloak. His crown wasn't the best, but his clothes were the finest that could be woven in Israel. He splayed the tassels and smoothed the lapels down to show off the blue embroidery.

The boy seemed like an average young man. Saul twisted the ends of his beard around his fingers. What had he been expecting? Beams of light shooting out of the boy's eyes? Wings like a heavenly being?

Sure, he was ruddy and handsome, and he had enough hair on his face to produce a shadow, which was good. Saul couldn't take a smooth-skinned child seriously.

The whispering in the room that had started up as soon as Saul returned to his throne swirled in his head like dry leaves. He itched to pull at his hair to get it to stop. But there was an easier solution. "It is time for you to leave the king alone."

The whispering stopped, but nobody left, so he repeated his words a little louder.

Still nobody moved.

"Out! Get out!" He lunged at a group of soldiers. "This is not a public entertainment. All of you, out. Now!"

They fled, even the singing shepherd. He had to send his oldest son, Jonathan, to run after the boy and bring him back.

The boy dropped to his knees and studied the floor as if he had never seen stones and plaster before.

"You're the reason they were all standing around in the middle of the day." Saul rubbed his fingertips against his royal mantle. "Did they tell you why you're here?"

"To sing for Adonai's Anointed."

Saul didn't hear any undercurrents of pity or mockery in the boy's answer. "Nothing else?"

"My lord?"

So he probably didn't know the whole story. His advisers felt free within Gibeah, but at least they were discreet enough not to blab about the king's spiritual condition to a nobody from nowhere. "Show me what you've got."

The boy took his lyre out of his bag and tested the strings—still on his knees.

"Your piety is noted, but you can get up now."

The shepherd blushed as he wobbled to his feet. "I'm not sure—" He looked from Saul to Jonathan, and back. "Where would Adonai's Anointed like me to play?"

Saul flicked his right hand. "Over here, over there, walk around, whatever you need. Start before I lose interest and," he muttered the end, "you lose your head."

The shepherd closed his eyes. His fingers hovered above the strings.

Saul gripped Jonathan's forearm. If this didn't work, his only alternative was to hope someone attacked them soon. On the battlefield, there was no time to be tormented by spirits.

But then the first notes hummed, soft and sweet. Saul leaned his head back against the wall, closed his eyes and breathed evenly for the first time in days.

"Father," Jonathan whispered.

Saul let go of Jonathan's arm and waved away whatever else his son was going to say. Whether *He* was with the boy, Saul had no idea, but this shepherd was no average musician.

"The earth is Adonai's and everything in it," the shepherd sang. "The world and all its people belong to Him."

The boy sang about *Him*, but it didn't bother Saul like it usually did. First, his jaw unclenched, then his shoulders.

> We praise You, Lord, for all Your glorious power.
> With singing we salute Your mighty acts.
> Some nations boast of armies and weapons.
> We boast in Adonai our God.
> Yes, we boast in Adonai our God.

Yes, mighty acts. There were mighty acts. Those were good times.

Saul angled his head nearer to Jonathan. "Remember what the Lord did to the Philistines at Micmash?"

"Made them panic until they were swinging their swords like blind men trying to kill bees." Jonathan laughed quietly. "How could I forget?"

Saul settled back and let the music wash over him.

> Honor Adonai for His glory and strength.
> Worship Adonai in the splendor of His holiness.

Saul motioned for the shepherd to come closer. The playing got louder as the boy approached.

"You will stay here and sing for me when I request it, except when I go to war." Saul opened his eyes. The boy was so young. "You don't belong on the front lines." And he didn't need soothing there. He closed his eyes again.

"Your father can take you back then. But for now, play. Play."

Saul hadn't felt this at peace since right after the first time Samuel anointed him, in the hills of Zuph, before anyone else knew, when it was just him and Adonai. This was the first time in moons he'd even been able to think, "Adonai," instead of "*Him*."

It wouldn't last. It never did.

So he enjoyed it while he could.

3. The fortress

David shrugged off whatever animal kept nosing his shoulder, but it wouldn't give up. A hand grasped his shoulder and shook it. Sheep couldn't do that. Goats couldn't do that. Someone whispered his name. Which was confusing. Nobody he knew would wake him either quietly or gently.

He slit open his eyes. He was in a room, curled up on his side on a stone floor with a wall at his back. A man squatted in front of him.

David rubbed the heel of his hand into his eyes before opening them again.

It was the man who stayed with King Saul yesterday.

The king.

The fog in his brain rolled away and he remembered everything: the trip to Gibeah, the sandstorm in his belly, the king making fun of him in front of everyone, and then playing nonstop until he collapsed in this spot and somehow kept going until the king fell asleep as the birds sang just before dawn.

David croaked a greeting, but the man hushed him.

"He's still asleep." The man put his finger against his lips and nodded toward an open doorway.

David pushed himself onto his elbow and shifted his

legs, wincing at the loud scuff of his sandals on the stone, but the king didn't stir. His feet prickled. When he put weight on them, he wobbled so hard he fell against the wall. The man had to hoist David up and help him hobble out of the room.

They left through a different doorway than he'd come in yesterday. This one led to a long dark room as wide as a donkey stall. It took ten steps for enough feeling to return to David's feet that he could walk on his own.

"My father hasn't slept this late or this soundly in days."

The sandstorm swirled inside David again. "Your father?"

"I'm Jonathan."

David gasped. How many times had he and the other boys in Bethlehem pretended to be Jonathan climbing the cliff at Micmash? Wait until he told Joab.

When would he be home next to tell anyone anything?

They walked in silence, still not all the way through the long room. What was this narrow room called? Why did it only have a packed earth floor? Why was there nothing in it? Where were they heading? Where would he sleep? How often would he play for the king? When could he eat? When and where could he relieve himself?

"Keep your head down and do as you're told without needing to know why."

He was most of a day's journey from home and he still couldn't escape his father.

"How old are you?"

The sudden question made David jump. "Fourteen."

Jonathan slipped through an opening in the wall and David followed him up the tower. The stairs stopped after the second floor, where stones stuck out of the sides like hand and footholds on a ladder. He climbed until his legs were as wobbly as a new lamb's.

After Jonathan reached the top and got out, David squinted against the sunshine that slanted down the shaft, hot and bright.

It must be full morning. At home, he'd have gotten such a beating if he ever slept past sunrise.

David scrambled up the last few stone holds and pulled himself out. He tripped and fell to the edge, his head and shoulders plunging through an opening before he caught himself. His vision swam and his stomach flipped. The ground was really, really far away. This wasn't the roof. They were on top of the lookout tower.

He put his arm around the square pillar to his right and hugged himself to it. The low part of the parapet reached his hip, and the regularly spaced pillars were taller than Eliab. The pillars must be where the archers would hide after they shot at the enemy.

The tower was as high above the city wall as a house. His father had told him about streams that dug deep crevasses into hills that went straight down like this, but he'd never seen one. It was very different than being on even the tallest hill at home.

He glanced at Jonathan. The king's son was so unfazed that he stepped up between the pillars and lifted his—

David looked away. The pressure in David's groin became almost unbearable when he realized what Jonathan was doing.

"When my brothers and I were your age, this was our favorite place to take our morning piss," Jonathan said. "It was a contest to see who could get over the wall. Once, Malchishua swore he hit that tree, but nobody else was there, so who knows."

David shifted his head so he could see the arc of liquid splash against the top of the wall below them. He gritted his teeth.

"Come on," Jonathan said. "I know you've got to go."

"If you were one of my brothers, you'd be doing this to get me in trouble."

Jonathan laughed. "How many brothers?"

David crossed one foot over the other and squeezed his thighs together. "Seven. All older."

Jonathan whistled. "Look around. There's nobody here who could object. Nobody can see us."

Indeed, they were at the back of the building, so nobody could possibly see what he was about to do.

He kept a death grip on the pillar as he stepped up, lifted his tunic and loincloth and let go. The last time he went had been right before he got to Gibeah yesterday after midday. It was such a relief that his toes and fingertips tingled.

Before he was even halfway done, he laughed, which made the stream wave about and splash against the tower. He got himself under control, but he was too shaky to get anywhere near the city wall like Jonathan had. He stifled a sigh as he lowered his clothes.

"Told you it was fun." Jonathan swung his arm in a wide arc. "Have you ever seen so far in your life?"

David shook his head as his gaze ranged over hills and spied a flock so distant that the sheep were the size of caper buds.

"There's Micmash," Jonathan said.

It didn't take much for David to imagine the armies camped out on opposite hills.

"And those are the cliffs, Bozez and Seneh."

A breathy "Wow" escaped David's lips before he could rein it in.

"Before my father was king, we lived in my grandfather Kish's household." Jonathan pointed to a large compound in the valley with its own low wall. "Those are his fields, and next to them are the king's fields, on this hill and the next one over."

At home, that was grazing land for the entire village.

"Let's head down to the roof." Jonathan jumped off the parapet.

David sat before hopping down. He hadn't eaten since yesterday midday and didn't entirely trust his body. They clambered down the hand and footholds on the outside of the tower.

From here, he could make sense of the building: it was a massive house with a chunk cut out of the middle for a courtyard. The double doors, almost as big as a city gate, which he'd come through yesterday, were in the middle of the front wall, opening to the courtyard. The tower was on the back corner, opposite from the room they took him to yesterday.

"Where are you from?" Jonathan asked.

"Bethlehem."

"Ever been in a gated city before?"

David shook his head.

"This was the Philistine governor's garrison until my father took it over, but anything you know about your hometown is the same here." Jonathan pointed outside the walls at a boy down the slope with sheep behind him. "Children still take the family sheep out every day." And then at a courtyard. "Women grind their grain and bake their family's bread every morning. And girls come back from the cistern with jars of water."

Jonathan strolled closer to the edge of the roof near the inner courtyard. "See how this part of the fortress looks different than that part over there?"

So that's what this was called: the fortress. David

looked across the open courtyard. That part was a little lower and its stone was more finely hewn.

"That was the house my father had built when he first became king, but when we couldn't get rid of the Philistines at Geba for so long, he added this wing and made it into a fortress with the big tower so we could better defend the city," Jonathan said. "The family quarters are above the receiving room. Soldiers stay on the second floor of where we're standing, domestic servants on the first."

They'd probably put him on the first floor of this building, with the servants. Would he get to meet the soldiers? How would he spend his time when not with the king?

Jonathan scratched the roof with his sandal. "You can see the inner and outer walls with filler stones in between. Super strong. But hard to put gaps in, which is why it's so dim all the time."

David meant to say "hmm," but it came out more like a groan.

"You get used to it." Jonathan didn't sound convinced.

It'd be a big change from being out with the sheep. Would he be inside all the time? Would the king make him play for that long every time? David pressed his finger pads against his thumbs, testing how tender they were.

Jonathan must have seen him grimace, because he took David's right hand and inspected it. "The army commander, Abner, has salve for that."

David tugged his hand free and curled his fingers in. Ask that hulk of a man for something for a few popped blisters? No.

"There's blood on your tunic."

David scrubbed the fabric with the heel of his hand, but after going through four brothers before him, the tunic was covered with as many stains as there were stars on a clear night.

"I heard you sing yesterday," Jonathan said. "So I know you are capable of speech."

In his world, the eighth son of a village family didn't joke around with the king's heir. David pretended not to hear him.

Jonathan shrugged and led David back down the tower into a large room that looked more familiar to him than any had so far. There were jars and bags of grain, piles of bread and cheeses, and mounds of dried figs and grapes: as much food as the entire town of Bethlehem spread out on the Festival of Final Harvest.

His stomach was too hollow to even grumble in hunger. They walked past all that food, out the doors to the cooking courtyard. Was nobody going to feed him? How often did servants eat? Would he have to work all day first?

The king's son headed for an older woman kneeling by a giant bowl, fluffing fat grains of cracked wheat.

It took all of David's discipline to hold himself back from jumping on that wheat and inhaling it.

"Mother, this is David of Jesse from Bethlehem."

She looked at him. "Our singer?"

"Yes, ma'am," David managed to whisper.

"We heard you through the windows last night." She sat back and licked a few grains of wheat off her fingers. "Where did you learn to sing like that?"

"I started singing to get the sheep to follow me."

Jonathan nudged him. "Better not let my father hear you liken him to your sheep."

David's stomach hollowed even more as he stammered.

"I'm kidding," Jonathan said.

"Leave the poor boy alone," Jonathan's mother said. "Your father is still asleep." She smiled.

But didn't offer any food. And David couldn't ask.

Jonathan grinned. "He is going to be the best thing that's happened to us since we trounced the Philistines last year."

She narrowed her eyes at David. "Those are your only clothes?"

"He's the youngest of eight sons and Father had him playing so long last night that his fingers bled."

"Do you have a mother?"

"Yes." It seemed like she was waiting for more, so he said, "Nitzevet of Adael."

"Doesn't she have anything better for you?"

"M-maybe." But it'd be impossible to get Father to give it up.

She sighed. "I'll have to rustle up something. You can't be associated with the king in something like that." She frowned at Jonathan. "Don't just stand there. Show him the servant quarters and then attend your father."

On their way back through the food storage room, David eyed a pile of raisin cakes, but wasn't near enough to palm one. Jonathan pushed aside the thick mat woven of rushes that separated two rooms. "Female servants on the right and male on the left."

The servants were somewhere else, but their sleeping rolls were laid out with small piles at the head.

"A messenger should be back before nightfall with the rest of your belongings."

This was happening. Someone had already been sent to Bethlehem to tell his parents and brothers that he was to serve the king. The first real and natural smile of the day spread across David's face. "Thank you, uncle."

Uncle? David flinched. How many more times would he embarrass himself here? At least Jonathan seemed not to notice.

And then David was alone. He had no bedroll to put down, nothing to arrange. What was his mother even going to send as "his belongings"? He tried to do the honorable thing and wait there for someone to come and tell him what to do, but nobody was in the storeroom, and it was full of food.

He darted out, grabbed as much as he could carry, and fell on it like a bear on the spring lambs.

What was wrong with the king that choosing not to eat or sleep was even possible?

4. Three moons later, fall 1026 bce

David was outside. With a flock. There were no walls to be seen anywhere. It wasn't yet the rainy season, so the sky was clear. The wind was hot and dry, but it was strong enough to blow out the stink of too many people stuck together for too long indoors, of human and animal waste, and of heavy smoke that had been lodged in his nose since he'd arrived.

It had taken days and days of working with the king's shepherds before the sheep and goats recognized his leadership enough to follow him. All he was doing was taking a small portion of the flock that stayed in Gibeah for the fall to a nearby well for watering, but he felt at home for the first time since leaving Bethlehem.

Unlike the king, the flock's needs were clear: water and safety. Unlike at the fortress, his job here was clear: guide the animals to the well; bring up water and fill the ground trough so they could drink; take them home. He knew how to do that like he knew how to chew and swallow his own food.

But he wasn't going to ruin this morning by thinking

about his strange life as the servant nobody knew what to do with. Instead, he looked up. And sang.

> The sun lives in the heavens where God placed it.
> It rejoices like an athlete eager to run the race.
> The sun rises at one end of the heavens and
> follows its course to the other end.
> Nothing can hide from its heat.

After his song had bounced around the hills, looping over itself like a tiny bird in the sky, he heard an echo that wasn't his. Someone else was in the hills.

"*Too much joy always brings disaster.*"

That was one of the worst of his father's sayings. How could he repeat that one to himself as if it were true? Because it wasn't. It couldn't be. There was too much disaster and not nearly enough joy, if you asked him. Which nobody did.

The other voice echoed again, closer this time, trailing off with the sound, "id, id, id." His name? Was someone calling him?

David stopped until one of the goats head-butted him. "Sorry, little one." He rubbed the long ears of the nearest sheep. "The last time someone came running into the hills to fetch me was less than two years ago. I got to meet the prophet Samuel. I don't know that this will be good news for me, though."

He scanned the terrain in the direction of Gibeah and

saw someone running in his direction. His name echoed again, more distinctly this time. Too soon, the man, another servant of the king, was there, breathing heavily from his run. "The king ... the king is calling for you."

David's knees buckled like a newborn lamb's. Of all the things he'd imagined someone needing him for, that hadn't occurred to him. "But it's during the day."

"What?"

"The king only asks for me at night."

"Well he needs you now. Go. I'm taking over the flock."

"Does the king know–"

"Shut up and run!"

David bolted. The fear in the other servant's voice spiked through him like a fever. He ran without thinking, because every time he worried about what the king would say or how the king would punish him, he stumbled, which meant that he'd get to Saul that much later.

His lungs were burning by the time the walls of the city came into view. There was only one entrance into Gibeah, so he had to skirt the hill to get to the road. Carmi, the household manager, was standing just outside the gates with David's lyre. David tried to take it mid-stride, but Carmi held onto it.

Once he was forced to stop, David doubled over, his hands on his knees, panting so hard, both from effort and from panic, that he couldn't get any words out, couldn't ask what had happened to change the only pattern he'd known at the fortress.

"Calm down," Carmi said. "You're no help to the king in this state, which means you're no help to the rest of us."

"Does the king," David finally managed to get out. "Does he know ... I just ... wanted ... to be useful?"

Carmi did not look reassuring. "Nobody can talk to the king when he's like this. All he knows is that you weren't here when he called for you."

David straightened and hugged the lyre to his chest when Carmi let go of it. "Did a tribal delegation arrive and nobody told me?"

His immediate answer was a cuff to the back of the head. "Are you blaming me?"

Nothing was going David's way. "No, my lord. Those are the times he calls for me: at night and after a tribal delegation leaves." It was the only thing he'd been able to count on since coming here three moons ago.

"He's the king." Carmi headed through the gates and David followed. "Get in there and work your sorcery."

David stopped. "It's not sorcery."

Carmi turned around and his eyes widened. "Stop arguing and get in there."

So David sprinted to the receiving room. It was already empty of people except for Saul. Not even the king's oldest son was there. Jonathan was the only other person who the king could bear to have with him when the demons were bothering him.

Saul slouched on his throne and stared out a window, his right hand opening and closing around the shaft of his spear. He didn't seem to notice that David had come in, so David dropped to both knees. "Please forgive me, my lord. I only wanted to be use–"

The king's gaze shifted and he met David's eyes for the first time since the day David arrived.

David flinched and jerked his gaze to the floor. How could eyes that cold feel like they'd burned him?

Saul spoke so quietly that David had to lean forward to hear him. "Do. Not. Ever. Be difficult to find."

Before David could get any reassurances or further apologies out, the king cut him off with a curt, "Play."

David risked a glance. The king was leaning back, eyes closed, spear across his lap–how he usually was while David played. Instead of standing, as *he* usually did, David sat; his legs were too tired to support him. His breath still came too fast and shallow to sing, so he picked his strings and wondered what story could help his king. When it came to him, he thanked Adonai for the inspiration, and spoke in a sing-song:

Oh, the prophets, when they praise,
they whirl like sand in a storm,
they leap like goats in the hills,
their arms wave like trees in the breeze.
Their joy in Adonai cannot be contained.
No, their joy cannot be contained.

Oh, the warrior, when he plots,
he is sly like the scorpion,
he is stealthy like the lion,
his aim is sure like the eagle.
His zeal for justice cannot be contained.
No, his zeal cannot be contained.

Oh, the tyrant when he laughs,
he is soon to be defeated,
he is about to be cut down,
By the warrior in prophet robes,
who whirled and leapt closer, and closer,
until knives flashed in his hands,
and the governor laughed no more.
Ha, ha, the governor laughed no more.

A snort came from the throne. David paused to see whether the king would add any commentary, but when none came, he peeked: the snort was a snore. The king was asleep. David hadn't even gotten all the way through one of his favorite stories, about how Saul, hiding among the prophets, kicked off the rebellion against the Philistine governor. He didn't even get to do his favorite line, "Is Saul a prophet?" It was a bit of a letdown after all the fuss to fetch him, but at least he didn't have to play until his fingers bled.

*****

The next day, David sat cross-legged on his bedroll, halfheartedly restringing his lyre. He hadn't budged from the servants' quarters, not even to help the other servants prepare the morning meal. They didn't say it out loud, but he could understand their thoughts as if they did: lazy, thinks he's so special, what good is he.

"David?" The household manager was calling him.

"Coming, Carmi." David jogged out to the kitchen courtyard.

"You've been moping around since—"

"Sorry. I'll do better." David wheeled around looking for something to do. If both the king and Carmi were upset, it might be worse for him than Eliab's worst days. He took a step toward the ovens and knocked over a pile of fuel patties. He dropped to a crouch and restacked them.

Carmi gave a heavy sigh. "The king gets angry with everyone. Snap out of it. If you want to be useful, take the soldiers in training their midday meal and then bring the serving implements back."

His throat clenched and he could barely swallow. This

was his first chance to see the soldiers training from close up. Why did it have to come when the king had ordered him to stay at the fortress? "Adonai's Anointed told me to stay here."

"The king is at the training," Carmi said. "If he needs you, you'll be right there."

David bit the edges of his tongue to stop himself from smiling. He popped to his feet. "I'd be honored."

His job was to carry a mountain of cracked wheat in a wooden bowl that hung over his outstretched arms by at least two handspans. The boys who carried sacks of bread had an easier time of it, swinging their bundles and skipping ahead of David, who had to step carefully. Still, he grinned the whole way down the path. His nephews back home were going to be so jealous.

They laid the food out under the pomegranate trees where the road leveled out. While they worked, the boys strained to catch glimpses of the army, but the trees blocked their view. Now it was David who had the advantage: all he had to do was put the bowl down, so he got to be the one to tell the officers that the meal had arrived.

He took his time.

There were thirty men David recognized, and about twenty he didn't. A group of men lined up behind the king, holding their shields in their right hands with weapons in their left. Why would they do that? Everyone knew it was supposed to be the opposite.

Then the king stood close to the right of the front man, and it made sense: they held their shields with their right hands so they could cover the king, leaving him free to fight with a weapon in each hand: Saul was training his armor bearers.

Abner stood up the hill a little and barked orders at the rest of the men. Most of them, including Jonathan, were working with bows, but a few used slings to fire at the straw targets. The slingers threw underhand, which, now that he saw them lined up together made sense. They'd get tangled up if they circled overhead.

David gasped. On a signal from Abner, they grunted in unison and switched the weapons from their right to their left hands. Some fumbled with their sling loop and some dropped their bows, but most of them hit the target as well as they had with the proper hand.

That was the most awesome thing he'd ever seen. He'd never even thought to switch hands. His fingers twitched. As soon as he wasn't needed, he was going to get his sling out and try it.

The boys behind him shouted and David startled. He'd almost forgotten that he had a job to do. "My lords! My lords! Food is here!"

Abner ordered the boys to gather the arrows and stones and pile them where the soldiers had been standing. They sprinted to the targets and yanked the arrows out of the straw, chattering nonstop about what they'd seen the soldiers do.

David went to the farthest target and dug his hand inside the straw to get the stones out. He checked the soldiers. They were all eating. None of them were paying attention to the boys. He dropped his armful of stones where the soldiers stood to fire and made sure nobody was watching before taking his sling off his belt and picking up several of those stones. To warm up, he let off a few with his right hand, using the same underhand throw the soldiers did. It put a lot less strain on his shoulder; he could see why they used it.

The other boys noticed what he was doing. The oldest one hissed at him to stop, but a few others egged him on. He switched the sling to his left hand. The loop didn't slip into place easily on his left middle finger, and the knot end felt as huge and unwieldy as a fist. The first time he spun the sling, the knot slipped out too soon and the rock skipped along the ground behind him.

His fellow servants laughed.

David did, too. It was harder than it looked. He tried again and, this time, managed to keep the sling together for several practice revolutions before letting the rock fly. It went way wide of the target, but it felt like success.

The boys clamored to have a turn, so he let them.

Before they realized it, Abner was on them. They jumped, but all he said was, "Fun's over."

As they cleaned up the eating area, David squeezed the big bowl into a sack and gathered the material tightly enough at the center of the bowl that he could hold it in front of him like a shield. Another boy brandished a serving spoon at him like a sword and they had a mini fight. The other boys grabbed what they could and did the same all the way up the hill.

That's how it was every day for fourteen of the best days of David's life, but then the extra men went back to their villages and David spent the two nights after that playing for the king until his fingertips bled and his voice was a bleat.

He was in the servants' quarters, oiling his lyre, when Carmi hustled him out to report to Jonathan. David went to the center courtyard and bowed. "Yes, my lord."

Jonathan held his bow and wore his arrow quiver. "Come with me."

"But the king–"

"Left for Gilgal this morning. I need someone to gather my arrows." Jonathan stalked through the fortress gates and David had no choice but to scramble to catch up.

When they got to the training field, Jonathan stopped at the first target and pointed David to the next one. "Go ahead. You were getting pretty good with your left. Don't want your skills to decline."

David stared dumbly at Jonathan. He couldn't have heard right. The king's son wouldn't invite him to train.

He stayed put. When Jonathan had shot all twenty-eight of his arrows, David found them and brought them back.

"I was serious," Jonathan said. "So long as you get my arrows when I ask, why not practice your own skills? Someday you'll use them for Israel."

When he put it that way, David couldn't come up with a reason why not. He gathered stones and then planted himself in front of the second hay target, where he alternated throws with his right and his left hands.

After Jonathan emptied his quiver twice, he challenged David to a distance competition. He shot first. It wasn't bad, but David had been throwing farther than that since he was eleven. Even so, he aimed at a spot near, but not past the arrow—he wasn't about to repay Jonathan's kindness by upstaging him.

"Not bad," Jonathan said. "I'd thought you could do better than that, but I forgot how young you are. I shouldn't have expected more from you." He sounded just like David's brothers when they goaded him and then punished him for taking them up on the dare.

David was too old to keep falling for that.

"Unless you're insulting the king's son by pulling back so he'll win."

Was Jonathan teasing him or threatening him? He didn't have enough experience with the king's son to be able to tell.

"You go first this time."

David sent up a silent prayer that Jonathan wasn't setting a trap for him. He planted his feet, bounced his knees a few times, and whipped that stone with all his strength. It soared past Jonathan's initial arrow. He held his breath.

Jonathan whistled. "Now *I'm* going to really try."

So he'd been teasing. David let out his breath with a relieved laugh and they tried to one-up each other until the sun was fully in the western sky. On their way back to the road, Jonathan led him near the last target. "I've got a surprise for you."

As if this day hadn't been unusual enough, Jonathan shifted some of the straw at the base and pulled out a shield. He turned it over, and the top and bottom edges flapped. "It's too cracked to use in combat, but you can practice with it, if you want."

If he wanted? David barely kept himself from snatching it out of Jonathan's hands and hugging it. His own shield.

"Keep it down here." Jonathan knelt to return it to its hiding place. "Tomorrow you can be my assistant again and we'll try it out against my sword."

David had never even daydreamed anything this good. It would only last until the king returned from his trip, but he'd be a fool if he didn't milk every chance he got.

5. Bethlehem. Six moons later, early spring 1025 bce

The army was arrayed behind the king and what seemed like all of Bethlehem was gathered in front of him. David stood in between, neither with the army nor with his townspeople.

King Saul stood under the same tamarisk tree by the threshing floor that Samuel had stood by three years ago. This time, the tree was raining pink petals that caught in the king's hair and on his shoulders, like a visible blessing from God.

"Men of Judah!" Saul's voice was loud and strong enough to carry over the crowd. "Proud warriors for the Lord's glory!"

The hair on David's arms stood on end.

"Your brothers in western Judah are being overrun by Philistine raiders. They cry for help before the heathens steal their birthright. Woe to those who let the pagan dogs gnaw on the bones of our brothers." Saul paused and looked over the crowd as if searching out those guilty of that crime. "Men of Bethlehem, take up your weapons and fight. Mothers of Bethlehem, feed your army. We need to reach Gedera by nightfall."

This was the King Saul David's father had told him stories about: the inspiring military leader who led the army into victory. It was easy to see how *this* man could unite Israel into one nation.

And then Bethlehem burst into activity. Women rushed home, counting on their fingertips or drawing figures in the air, calculating how much they could give away while still feeding their families until the first grain harvest. Sons and fathers clustered together, negotiating who would go with the army and who would stay behind to work the fields and the hills.

David shouldered through the chaos looking for his family. Finally, he and Shimea spotted each other.

His brother called over everyone's heads, "Father's finally letting me join!"

David yelled his congratulations and headed east through town, weaving to avoid the people carrying jars and sacks of grain and stacks of bread and cheeses to the army. He clipped one woman's bundle and scrambled to catch her breads before they hit the ground.

The woman scolded him. She sounded familiar. When he straightened, he saw why. "Zeruiah."

"Oh, David. You're here. Take this, too." His sister plunked the cheese on top of the breads he was already bobbling in his arms.

He stabilized the pile with his chin and they joined the stream of women and children carrying food.

"I saw Shimea," David said.

"He's old enough to go now, isn't he?"

David nodded, which made him lose that cheese. He did a deep knee bend, keeping his back straight, so he could pick up the fallen cheese and not lose everything else. "Is Joab around?"

"Somewhere. Probably trying to look older so he can sneak away to fight."

David grinned. At least Joab hadn't changed.

They delivered the food to the supply manager.

"Go help Mother." Zeruiah waved him away without looking at him.

This time, David skirted the outside of town to get home. Home. Despite nine moons in Gibeah, Bethlehem was still that.

He skidded down the pebbled slope a bit when he saw his house. His father and brothers had added a wing; that must mean he had more nieces and nephews. Even so, it seemed small and vulnerable with no high walls, although the sheep's bleating when he approached kind of worked like soldiers raising the alarm.

"Quiet, animals," his mother yelled. "I can't concentrate."

"Mother!" David was overrun by wooly and bristly animals butting his legs. He turned his hands palms out for the flock to nose as he made his way to the house. "You remember me?" he crooned to them. "Of course you do. Because you naughty creatures need to go back into your fold. How did you get out? Where are the rest of you?"

He led them back into their enclosure and used his foot to set the rolling stone back in place.

His mother was in the house. She didn't notice him, not while he was gathering the flock and not even when he dropped his pack inside the doorway. He'd been gone for so long, and not one person greeted him. Not even his own mother.

He pressed his thumb against his eyebrow to ease the pressure behind his eyes. "Mother, I'm here to help."

She bustled about, her tunic flapping between her calves. "Finally. Load up the yoke with those bags of grain and take them to the army, and then rush back for the wine jar. These fig cakes are not cooperating."

David did as he was told and was passing the oven in the yard when his mother drew up even with him.

"Oh!" She swatted his arm. "David. It's you. You're back." She pulled him close and kissed his cheeks.

He was too old for that, but if it made her feel better, he wasn't going to argue.

"Let's get these to the army and then we can give you a proper greeting and hear all about life with the king. Unless you're going with them? But no, you're too young. Too young, I say."

He twisted out of her grasp and walked on. "Don't worry, I'm not going."

"Oh, good. The oldest three are one thing, but not you. Not yet."

His mother went on and on, talking about "her baby" and analyzing the state of the hair on his face. The patches had to connect soon. Maybe then he'd get some respect.

They met his fourth oldest brother heading back to the house. He didn't notice David, either.

"Nethanel," his mother said. "Get the wine jar. It's the last thing. And hurry."

The grain was getting heavier, the yoke digging into David's shoulders, but he trudged on. Even after he dropped the bundles on a supply cart, he could still feel the pressure.

He stood back with his mother and watched while the army finished its midday meal and rose on Abner's command, but not as one—they were nothing like the well-oiled troops who trained year-round in Gibeah.

Abner called out, "The Lord our God."

Some of the men answered, "The Lord is one!"

The commander had to repeat it twice, his voice a more threatening growl each time, before Judah's troops gave him a properly rousing and unified response.

David and a crowd of boys followed the army as far as

the well outside of town and watched them head south until they disappeared from sight.

"That was awesome!"

"Nobody can beat our army."

"I can't wait until I can join."

"We'll show those Philistines."

But David didn't join the boasting as the boys headed back to town, because all he could think was, *this is the army*? Knowing how the army was raised and seeing it happen were two very different things. The Benjaminites who stayed in Gibeah year-round and trained with Abner and iron weapons were impressive. But they were a minority. The tribal army was mostly farmers and shepherds armed with axes, slings, and the occasional scythe that was probably too dull to cut grain properly. Most of them wore handed-down armor made of layers of wool glued together with a goat skin stuck on top of that.

Adonai had better be with them. Otherwise, they didn't stand a chance.

His father was alone in the house when David got there.

Jesse rested his hands low on his hips. "About time. And no more dawdling with the little boys. If you're home, you're home to work."

David rolled his shoulders. "Yes, my lord."

"Is the king unhappy with you?"

"No, my lord. He doesn't want underage people on the battlefield."

"You're criticizing the king's judgment?"

One look from his father made the back of David's neck burn. "My music could be inspiring for the troops. When I play for–"

Jesse snorted. "You are that full of yourself that you think a little plinking of the strings would make a difference in a war?"

David stammered. That wasn't it. Or, at least not all of it. There had to be some bigger reason Samuel had anointed him. Being Saul's favorite musician didn't seem...enough.

"All that playing your lyre has make you soft." Jesse grabbed David's arm and pulled him toward the sheepfold. "Some good, honest work will cure that."

"Yes, my lord." David couldn't help flexing his muscles so his father would know how wrong he was.

Jesse chuckled and let go. He got to the sheepfold ahead of David, but instead of walking through, he picked up a club that leaned against the wall. "Don't repeat this to your brothers, but you've brought honor to our family."

David stopped in his tracks, the back of his throat thickening.

"Again." Jesse tapped the club on the ground. "Do you ever think about that old prophet, Samuel?"

Only every day. "Sure."

"Do you know why he anointed you?"

This was the first time his father had asked straight out. David shook his head.

"You haven't heard from the Lord?"

"Not about that."

Jesse narrowed his eyes. "About what?"

David's heart thumped. "Nothing specific. I sense Him telling me to play certain songs at certain times, and I–" He took a quick breath for courage. "I feel His pleasure when I play."

He'd never admitted that before. People talked a lot about Adonai's power and might, and His blessings for His people, but not about His pleasure in them specifically.

"Well." Jesse's gaze slid away until he was looking up the hills. "Your fool brother Ozem left the flock in the fields. As if seeing the army will make up for losing our livelihood. Go help him gather those who didn't make their way back."

Even though his heart was still pounding, a run into the hills sounded good.

"Try the northwest first. And take this," Jesse held the club out to David. "The lions have gotten two of the late lambs this week."

David grasped the club and headed out.

He was *not* soft. He swung at a bit of scrub and sent the new growth flying.

And it was *not* easy to play for the king. His shoulders

constantly ached from being hunched over and his fingers often bled from playing for so long. Another swing and more leaves sprayed the air.

Maybe if that was all he did, he would've turned into a weakling, but he had all that secret army training. If anything, he was tougher than when he'd left home last year.

He finally found Ozem to the east of town.

"Go away!" Ozem yelled. "Get lost!"

David kept coming. He'd been given a job and he was going to do it, no matter who objected.

Ozem was madly pointing to David's right.

And then he saw it.

A lion.

It was between them. When it turned its head and snarled at David, the high notes lodged in the base of his scalp and sent shivers down his spine.

"Let her take a lamb!" Ozem waved him away. "We have plenty."

Why had he left his sling in his pack? He could have used that precision distance weapon. But he'd never lost an animal on his watch. His brothers were always losing lambs and kids, either just plain losing them or letting wild animals get them. David was not that kind of shepherd. He tightened his grip on the club.

If Ozem stayed where he was, between the lion and the flock, David could try the flanking maneuver he'd watched the army practice. He crouched and edged to the side until he could still see it, but it couldn't see him. The animal was surveying the remnant of the flock, waiting for her opening. Ozem ran for cover behind a rock. So much for flanking.

The flock could smell a predator. They knew something was wrong, but nobody was leading them or trying to keep them safe.

The lion's front shoulders were rotating; she was getting ready to run. David sprinted, but she took off before he got near. The lion scattered the flock. She was faster than David, but he found he could anticipate her moves. The lion ran in an arc after some sheep heading for higher ground, and David moved to cut her off, but then the lion yelped and twisted in the air.

Ozem circled his sling above his head. At least his brother was doing something. Another stone hit the lion's back flank, but she ignored it. She was too close to a lamb, a perfect white one. One lunge and she engulfed it.

6. Playing at war

A heartbeat later, David launched himself at the lion, rolling her to the ground and setting the lamb free.

The lion rose. David's legs were hooked around her torso and his left arm around her neck, so he went up with her. She swung her head from side to side, her jaw snapping on air. Then she dropped on him and writhed in the dirt.

As long as he stayed on her back, she didn't have a good angle to get at him with her claws or her teeth, but her frenzied attempts made it hard for David to do anything but hold on. It wasn't until she tired that he could free his arm to swing up and smash the club onto her head.

Her scream was unearthly, but she was stunned enough that he could grab her lower jaw to steady her head and keep at her with the club until the struggle left her body and his own heavy panting was the only sound David could hear.

Blood and bits of flesh spattered his club, his tunic, the side of his face. His left hand, still under her jaw, was hot and sticky. The lion's powerful body was still warm.

David closed his eyes. "Thank you, Lord."

He had to tug his tunic free before he could stand. By the time he did that, Ozem was whooping and hollering.

David's legs shook like stalks of wheat in a windstorm. He'd just wrestled a lion. When he'd killed predators before, it had been at a distance, with a stone from his sling. Shouldn't he feel powerful or excited? Shouldn't he feel something?

"I can't believe you did that! You're crazy!"

David held up his hands before Ozem got any closer. "I've got dead animal all over me. You don't want to be unclean, too."

Ozem laughed. "Seriously? Wait 'til I tell Father you killed a lion with your bare hands–"

"And my club. And the Lord."

"Whatever. Wash up in the yard. You'll be fine."

This wasn't about the mess. It was about righteousness. "Unclean isn't the same as dirty."

Ozem rolled his eyes. "Do what you want. I'm taking the rest of the flock back and telling Father and we'll break out the wine whether you're there to enjoy it or not."

David wiped himself off as well as he could with some grass and dirt, and helped Ozem gather the animals. If only his lyre wasn't in his pack back at the house, so he could play to calm the poor creatures down.

The injured lamb was moving about but limping. He pinned it between his knees and inspected it. Small holes from the lion's teeth produced some blood, but it hadn't gotten seriously chomped, so it would probably survive.

David gathered it in his arms, holding it tightly so it wouldn't squirm loose and injure itself further.

"Leave it behind," Ozem said.

David ignored him.

Ozem poked a sheep with his staff. "For once in your life, can't you *not* be noble?"

What was he supposed to say to that? He kept walking, singing quietly to the lamb.

Ozem kept up a sulky silence until they were halfway home. "So what does a king do all day, anyway?"

"Depends." The lamb was getting heavy, so David slung it around his shoulders. "Some days he spends a lot of time with Abner and the army, training with his armor bearers. Other days, he gets visitors from other tribes who bring tributes."

Ozem snorted. "You mean taxes."

"Of course. A moon ago, leaders from Gad came with seven calves, dozens of birds, sack after sack of grain, a hundred cheeses, I don't even know how many gallons of wine, and ten huge men. The men of Benjamin put on an archery show, all of them switching to their left hands halfway through, and the men from Gad showed off their spear and shield skills and then there was a huge feast."

"And you got to go?"

David shifted the lamb to cradle it again. "I wish."

The house was in sight, which was good, because this

little lamb felt as heavy as a full sack of grain, except that sacks of grain didn't try to squirm away.

"Is King Saul as big as they say?"

"I come up to his shoulder. Eliab would be at his nose."

"I'd love to see someone get away with looking down on Eliab." Ozem sighed. "So do you just sing?"

Oh, the contempt Ozem poured into the word *sing*. "I can't even count the number of times I've played from dinner to breakfast. Have you ever stayed up all night?" He didn't add, "without food or drink or relieving yourself?"

Ozem shoved a sheep away from his leg. "During lambing season. Or have you already forgotten?"

"Well you don't have to worry about whether the sheep will get annoyed with you and run you through with a spear."

For a moment, Ozem looked like he was going to argue that something about shepherding was more dangerous than that.

It was so tempting to describe what it was like when evil spirits tormented the king, but David didn't want to speak ill of Adonai's Anointed. Especially not now, while the king led three of their brothers off to war. Even what he said about the spear was probably a mistake.

When they were in sight of home, Ozem thrust his staff into David's hand and ran ahead. "I can't wait to tell everyone."

"It's my story!"

Ozem ran backwards. "I'll tell it better."

"You mean you'll make yourself sound better!" David yelled. "You're leaving the flock again."

When he neared the house his young nieces and nephews burst out, talking over each other. "Uncle David, is it true?" "Did you really kill a lion?"

David stepped behind the biggest goat. "Stop! Stay away. I've got dead animal all over me."

The older ones wrinkled their noses and slowed down, but looked him over and pointed out the gory bits to each other. The younger ones thought it was a game of chase and David had to keep dodging as they dove for him. "Seriously. Go back to your parents." Was it because he was laughing and juggling the lamb while he said it that they didn't obey?

He begged the older ones to help. They herded the young humans while David ushered the flock into their fold. He followed them in and rolled the stone between him and his family.

Once on its feet, the lamb scampered off, shaking its injured leg. "There you go, little fellow. No longer unblemished, but whole."

He inspected his left hand, the one that had been in the lion's mouth and covered with its blood. The blood had gathered in every crease and dried to a crusty, reddish brown studded with lamb fluff. David hid his hand behind his back and faced his family.

His nephews and nieces gathered around Ozem, clamoring for details, while he mimed the action, retelling the story so he tossed dozens of stones at the lion and struck it with his staff.

His remaining brothers, Nethanel and Raddai, and the oldest brothers' wives laughed at Ozem and challenged the truth of his version of the story.

David's mother stood by the oven in the yard, shaking her finger at him, her mouth moving, but he couldn't hear her. Wisps of steam poured out of a pot and curled around her. Steam meant food.

David's stomach made the same low growl as the lion. He swayed and tried to cover it by propping his right foot on a crevice in the wall and striking a confident pose.

"Show-off!" someone shouted from behind the family.

They turned around and David went up on his toes to see his accuser.

"Always boasting," the voice continued.

By then, David knew: it was his nephew and best friend.

A smiling Joab broke through. "You go off to live with the king and then when you come back you kill a lion with your bare hands. How are the rest of us supposed to compete with that?"

David grinned and shrugged.

Joab made to vault over the wall, but David backed away.

"Mr. Holier-than-the-rest-of-us is 'unclean,'" Ozem said in a sing-song.

Nethanel grunted. "I'm not waiting until he gets home from the spring to eat. The rest of us shouldn't have to suffer because our water isn't good enough for him."

David blinked several times. He could usually count on Nethanel to be fair, if not kind to him.

"This isn't a new moon festival or ritual feast," Nethanel said. "It's a normal dinner. Half of us aren't even here." He spat on the ground.

Jesse took two steps closer to Nethanel. "Not your call."

"Nothing is," Nethanel muttered before glaring at David. "Things were better when you were gone." He stalked back to the house and slammed the door behind him, his wife following quietly.

Nobody contradicted him or said that wasn't true. David didn't know where to look, so he stared at the trough until his vision blurred.

"Don't take it personally," Joab finally said under his voice. "Your father wouldn't let him fight because his wife just had a baby."

"She did?"

"You've been gone for over nine moons."

It was good to know what was behind Nethanel's outburst, but it didn't stop his chest from feeling scraped out. His mother walked over and David couldn't take his eyes off the dried fig cakes on a leaf in her right hand.

"What was that all about?" Nitzevet asked.

Nobody replied.

"Then what are you all standing around here for? Go make some fresh bread." She directed her daughters-in-law and they scurried to the oven. "Go ... go make yourselves useful." She shooed everyone but Joab and Jesse away. "Everyone fussing because David is doing the right thing, doing what we've taught him."

She clucked her tongue and put the two cakes on the rolling rock. "Take these when you go to the spring. Joab, go get David some fresh clothes so he can wash that blood off what he's wearing."

Joab ran into the house and his mother followed.

That left his father.

David eyed the food longingly.

Jesse crossed his arms. "You don't have to keep taking risks to prove you're as strong as your brothers."

David clenched his left hand behind his back. That wasn't it at all. He took down that lion because it was his job to protect those in his charge. With Adonai's help he was *better* than his brothers, who let predators have their way. "The Lord was with me."

"Of course." Jesse turned back to the house and yelled at someone to get a move on. David was dismissed.

He wanted to shout at his father's back, "Ritual washing

after touching a dead animal is one of the Lord's requirements, not suggestions. Requirements!" But he didn't. He crouched and gobbled up first one fig cake and then the other without touching them with his hands. They must have been at the end of their storage time, because they glued his jaw together., but the honey made them as sweet as manna. He probed his teeth with his tongue to get the seeds out and set off for the spring to the southwest of town.

Joab caught up with David on the main road.

"O, revered uncle, I have your clothes."

"You're only three years older," David said. "When are you going to get tired of that gag?"

"When you're older than me."

David put his palms together and shook them at the heavens. "Please, Lord."

Joab shouldered him sideways. "Someone said that the king has been training some men of Benjamin all winter. That true?"

David nodded.

"Man. You get to hang out near the army, see their weapons, watch them train. You get all the luck."

David shrugged.

"Details. I need details." Joab held his bundle out in front of him. "I'll drop your clothes right here and make you walk back naked if you don't tell me something soon."

"Okay, okay." David laughed. "Fifty or so men from Benjamin live in Gibeah and train year-round. Commander Abner hopes it'll grow when the tribes see the success of an army more like the armies we're fighting against. We'll never again scatter in fear because an army lines up in ranks against us."

Joab drove his right fist into his left palm with a satisfying smack. "Oh yeah."

"He's arranged them into units. Each unit has slingers and archers who fire from behind, archers in the way back and slingers close enough to aim at the enemy. Then the hand combat soldiers come in with spears and swords and daggers and anything that will hold an edge or has some heft for skull bashing."

"Who has the better weapons, us or the Philistines?"

"Philistines, for sure. We still don't have any metal forgers and it's not like the Philistine blacksmiths are going to make iron swords for their enemy. Their weapons are vicious."

"You've seen them?"

David smiled. Joab sounded so awestruck and jealous. "A few soldiers showed me their plunder. Long swords–"

"Not curved?"

"No," David said. "And get this–they keep an edge on both sides. Spear tops are so hard I couldn't dent them with a rock, but sharp enough to slice a ripe fig without crushing it."

Joab whistled. "What about chariots?"

"The king has some chariots, stolen from our enemies, of course."

"I didn't see any."

"They stay on the main roads. Local ones are too rough."

"I'd give anything to see the king ride into battle on his chariot." Joab stood tall, holding an imaginary spear.

"You won't."

Joab bristled. "Yes, I will. Someday I'll be old enough to go in the army–"

"Not that," David said. "He doesn't ride into battle on a chariot."

"Why not? Our enemies do. How are we supposed to fight against men on chariots unless we use them, too?"

David pushed at a pretend opponent. "Get the men off the chariot and they lose the advantage."

"But by the time you've gotten close enough to push the guy off, you're also close enough to be dead."

"We don't need to get close. Abner plans to stay in the hills and in the woods, where chariots are useless. To get at us, our enemies have to come to the hills at some point." David didn't like how puffed up he sounded. This was all stuff he'd overheard when nobody was paying attention to him, but how he said it made it seem like Abner had discussed these things with a barely fourteen-year-old.

"I can't believe the stuff you get to do, the people you get to meet."

"I wouldn't go that far," David said. "Abner has no idea who I am."

Joab made a skeptical noise. "Everyone who hears you play knows who you are."

David flicked a bit of lion flesh off his tunic. "The king kicks everyone out of the room before he asks for me."

"Strange."

"You have no idea," David murmured.

They left the road and headed up to the spring, the still-green grass tickling David's ankles.

Out of the blue, Joab asked, "How many villages did you stop in before Bethlehem?"

"None." David inhaled deeply. There must be mint under their feet. "Jonathan headed west to hit more villages before heading south."

"Was Abner yelling at the army the whole way here?"

David smiled. "Oh, you mean how he talks?"

Joab nodded.

"He always sounds that gravelly."

Joab deepened his voice and added a rasp. "When the king says move it he means now."

David laughed. "Not bad. I bet that's how he talked when he and Saul were young."

"I can't imagine that."

"They're cousins, so they must've run around together."

"Cousins you say." Joab stroked his short beard. "A nephew is way closer than a cousin. If you're ever king, swear an oath that you'll make me the commander of your army."

They'd reached the spot where the water bubbled out, so David stripped off his clothes. "You're funny." He sank to his knees and cleaned the fabric, glad that he didn't get lion's blood all over the tunic from the king's wife.

"You've never once imagined what it'd be like to be king?"

David used the wet cloth to scrub the dried blood from his skin before he lay face down in the swampy grass.

"Seriously. Swear it."

David turned over and closed his eyes, letting the water seep under and around him. "If I were king, I'd follow what the Lord told me to do. If He told me to put my smelliest and hairiest relative in charge of the army, I'd do it. Otherwise..."

Something heavy and cold landed on David's chest. He reared up and wet gravel plopped onto his lap. He scrambled upright, scraped up some mud and tossed it at Joab, who dodged David's lobs every time. After a few losing bouts, David put his hands up in surrender, and they both doubled over, laughing.

"Royal service is making you soft," Joab said.

"Nah. Chasing after Asahel is making you faster."

They were still laughing as David put the clean clothes on. They were warm from the sun and smelled like home.

As they walked back to the village, they weighed the merits of various weapons and retold old battle legends until David said, "But our best weapon is the Lord. Only He can throw a whole army into confusion so they kill each other and all we have to do is watch and then reap the plunder."

"See, that's why you'd make a great king," Joab said. "You say stuff like that and even I want to follow you into battle."

"Did a fever boil your brain while I was gone?"

"I'm serious."

David pointed at the olive tree ahead of them. "You'd follow that tree if it meant you could be a soldier."

Joab sniggered. "You've got me there."

"Besides, Saul has sons, and at least one of them is–"

"I know, I know. The elders still tell the story every time they get together. Jonathan and his armor bearer climbed up behind Philistine lines in the night and slayed them right and left." Joab acted it out. "Have you met him?"

"Do you promise to never tell anyone in my family, or in yours? Especially not my brothers," David said. "Do you swear it?"

"I promise."

"Be serious."

"Have I ever told on you? Not that you ever did much to tell about."

David poked him. "He's the older brother I never had."

That made Joab hoot. "You have nothing but older brothers."

"True, but Jonathan doesn't twist my ears or push me around or try to get rid of me. He gave me a tour of the fortress. When he noticed me hanging around and watching the army, he even gave me an old shield to practice with."

Joab went still. "Did you bring it with you?"

David shook his head. "It's safe in its hiding place in Gibeah."

"Must be nice." Joab walked on, his shoulders hunched.

"I'm not supposed to have it," David said.

"But, still, your own shield and you're only fourteen."

"A cracked and beat-up thing that was going to the burn pile. It isn't much better than the shields we used to weave out of grasses."

"You don't have to lie to make me feel better," Joab said.

David twisted his mouth. "It's true. Why do you think we always have to rely on the Lord? Our equipment stinks."

Joab gave a vicious kick to a stone in his path.

What kind of idiot was he to put down the army right after it marched off with half the village?

"Is this how the commander of my army behaves?" David asked. "Commander!"

"Huh?"

David pulled himself up to his full height, what there was of it. "I said, 'Commander!'"

Joab finally got it. He dipped his head. "Yes, my lord."

"Demonstrate for the rest of our troops how to properly skewer a Philistine."

"Gladly, my lord." Joab snapped a tall dry white broom stalk from the ground and held it at his shoulder. "Use your strongest arm, your right arm, for the spear. Your shield is looped around your left forearm so you can hold a smaller weapon in that hand. Use a dagger as a defensive weapon, jabbing, slicing. Swing an axe up at the face or punch it straight at the nose." Joab demonstrated each move as if the enemy were in front of him. "When you have him distracted enough, thrust forward with the spear. Aim for his collarbone to get between the helmet and his breastplate. If that doesn't work, then aim for his side, especially his armpit."

"There you are," Nitzevet called from the door of the house. "Stop playing at war and come in already."

The sun was behind the highest hill.

"Yes, Mother!" David sped up.

Joab did, too. "I can't wait to hear the story of the lion."

"Tell you later. I'm sure Ozem doesn't want me to tell the real version."

"Come on." Joab whined.

David paused at the front gate. "I don't want to end up like our ancestor Joseph. His older brothers weren't too happy when he got all the attention."

"Eliab's not here. Ozem doesn't have the courage to sell you into slavery, and Raddai always liked you. Besides, they'd have to get through me and my brothers first." Joab thumped his own chest. "And you know nobody can run fast enough to escape Asahel, even if he is only ten."

David appreciated Joab's confidence but couldn't bring himself to share it. Based on his family's reactions to his return, he was a burden, a pain, and another mouth to feed. Killing that lion wasn't making things any easier. He'd get through it now like he did after the anointing: take to the hills as much as possible. This time, he added: keep out of Nethanel's way and pray for the war to be over soon so the king could send for him again.

7. Gibeah. Eight moons later, fall 1025 bce

Saul wandered aimlessly around the nearly empty receiving room. Only his sons and Abner and his armor bearer were there. Jonathan was the best of his sons. Saul had once stood that tall and strong, that sure of his place in the world, but then Samuel came and ruined it. "Why doesn't it last?"

He hadn't meant to say that out loud.

Jonathan must have heard him, because he walked closer. "Why doesn't what last?"

"Anything good."

Jonathan's face was too composed.

Saul hated that cautious look. "I suppose you're going to call for that shepherd boy."

"I'd never do such a thing without asking, Father."

"Maybe not." Saul played with the ends of his beard. "But I bet the boy is in the fortress and I don't have to wait for him to arrive from his father's."

Jonathan didn't deny it. "He's not exactly a boy anymore."

"Is he married? Does he have children?"

"No."

"Boy." Saul let the silence play out until Jonathan took a deep breath, as if building up the courage to speak. "You think I need him right now, is that it?"

"It was a great victory against Zobah." Jonathan spoke as if reading each word as it was being written on the floor. "That was wise to gather the army from East Manasseh, where the men know how to fight in the desert."

"Costly for our men from Benjamin, though."

Jonathan nodded. "With all the men home and so many families in mourning, there isn't much work around here. What's the harm in enjoying some music?"

There was no harm, of course. Saul had been about to call for the boy, but he didn't like other people implying he needed to. Then again, if he didn't call for the boy out of spite, he'd only be punishing himself. "Get on with it, then. Send him in."

He headed for his throne, but was still a few steps away when he heard strings being plucked. Saul wanted to punch Jonathan for his presumption, but the music was already working.

"Go away, all of you." Saul assumed his listening position. "Your thoughts are making too much noise."

He tilted his head from side to side to stretch his sore neck and then opened his eyes a sliver to make sure they had all left.

Jonathan was right: the singing shepherd wasn't a mere boy anymore. He was taller and stronger than when he'd first come into service. Saul sighed and shut his eyes again. Soon the boy would want to join the army, and then he'd probably get killed, and Saul would be deprived of his music.

That's the way life was. Everything good ended.

But for now, he could let the song wash over him.

> Give praise to Adonai. Proclaim His name.

Saul flinched, like he did every time he heard *His* name. But after a few verses, he could hear the name without reacting. The boy always sang about *Him*.

> Tell the nations what He has done.
> Sing to Him. Sing praise to Him.
> Tell of all His wonderful acts.

"'*His* wonderful acts,'" Saul muttered. "Let me tell you of *His* wonderful acts."

The music became hushed and the boy stopped singing, as if he were waiting for Saul to tell him stories.

Saul had no intention of doing so. He was merely amusing himself with some sarcasm. "Keep going."

> He stands by His covenant forever,
> the promise He made
> for a thousand generations.

"Didn't you forget a verse?" Saul frowned.

The boy cleared his throat. "Remember the wonders He has done, His miracles, and the judgments He pronounced...."

So the boy tried to leave out a verse about *His* judgments. He couldn't know about–

No. Saul wasn't going to think about that anymore.

> He stands by His covenant forever,
> the promise He made
> for a thousand generations,
> the covenant He made with Abraham,
> the oath He swore to Isaac.
> He confirmed it to Jacob as a decree,
> to Israel as an everlasting covenant:
> "To you I will give the land of Canaan."

"Give?" Saul snorted. "There was very little giving. We paid for that gift with our blood. We're still paying for it."

> For He remembered His holy promise
> given to His servant Abraham–

"Stop changing it. Sing the Egypt part." Especially the plagues. The water into blood, the frogs, the flies, the locusts. As badly as Saul had messed up, he hadn't been punished *that* severely.

The boy went through all the plagues, but then he sang two lines over and over.

> He opened the rock and water gushed out.
> It flowed like a river in the desert.

By the third time Saul heard it, peace trickled through him like that river in the desert.

He closed his eyes again. If he focused hard enough, maybe he'd figure out how to bring this feeling back on his own, without needing the boy's music.

> A river reviving a dead and dry place.

That was exactly what it was like. Saul should know. He'd been in such a place for so long. "It hasn't always been dead and dry."

The music got quiet and Saul found himself talking.

"It had such a silly start. I was plowing and my father sent me to find some donkeys that had wandered away. Donkeys. Stupid creatures.

"I tramped all over Benjamin and Ephraim. Nothing. My servant gets the idea to ask a seer. It was Samuel, of course. There was a sacrifice that day. He brought me to the great hall and put me in the place of honor and gave me the choice cut of meat. He told me about my donkeys, even though I hadn't mentioned them to him."

Saul's laughter sounded hollow even to him. "The next day, he poured oil over my head, kissed my cheek, and told me I was to be leader of all Israel. I didn't believe him, so he told me the things that would happen to me. All the signs—the men at Rachel's tomb who told me the donkeys were found, the men with goats, bread and wine, and the band of prophets who gave me the idea for my first military success—they all came true."

And what a perfect day it had been. *His* spirit had changed everything about Saul. Things were so good. For a while.

Saul scratched his fingernails against the stone of his throne. "I kept it a secret. They would've laughed at me." He put on a nasally tone. "'Why would our first king come from tiny Benjamin?'"

The boy's strumming became more insistent, like a drumbeat, and the song had a rollicking tune:

> The word came to him while he plowed his field:
> Our brothers in Jabesh are besieged.
> Anger burned bright in Adonai's Anointed.
> "Rise up," he cried. "Rise up and fight."
>
> No nation can stand against Adonai our God.
> The Ammonites never had a chance.
> They fell at once to Adonai's Anointed.
> "Rejoice," Samuel cried. "Rise up and rejoice."

The song should have made Saul proud, but it only reminded him of what came after. "Then why did Samuel go on about how the people had sinned by asking for a king? I stood there like a fool while he said that the Lord may have chosen me, but He didn't want me. I had to suffer through that insult twice, once at Mizpah and once at Gilgal."

The boy barely made any noise with his lyre.

"What, you can't come up with anything to sweeten the king's bitterness?"

Saul hadn't expected an answer, but soon, he heard the boy singing softly, each note drawn out.

> O Lord, how long will You forget me?
> How long will You look the other way?
> How long must I struggle
> with anguish in my soul,
> with sorrow in my heart every day?

Pain threatened to double Saul over.

"Restore the light to my eyes," the boy sang. "Or I will die."

Saul choked back a sob.

> The law of Adonai is perfect,
> reviving the soul.
> The commandments of Adonai are right,
> bringing joy to the heart.
> They are more desirable than gold,
> even the finest gold.
> They are sweeter than honey,
> even honey dripping from the comb.

Saul could almost see the gold and taste the honey. He pleaded for their sweetness to overpower the bitterness in his soul.

It was a losing battle, almost worse than if he hadn't gotten any relief from the boy's singing at all.

But then the boy sang the opening to the Shema. "Hear O Israel, Adonai our God, Adonai is one." He sang it over and over, until Saul joined him.

The first time, Saul stumbled over His name, the intimate name. It had been so long since he hadn't merely mouthed it, but each time he and the boy sang it together, Saul pronounced it more clearly, until he surged to his feet and ran to the door. "Everyone, come now. Sing with us!"

He kept at his advisers until they had brought everyone in the fortress together, no matter how lowly or how important they were. As their combined voices washed over Saul, he knew they were one, the people with each other and Adonai with His people.

Saul slipped out and up the stairs to his quarters and fell asleep to the praises of the people.

8. Bethlehem. Three moons later, late winter 1024 bce

Uncle Jonathan leaned his elbows on the stone fence. "Didn't we just get rid of you?"

David knew his uncle was teasing, but it was exactly the response he was expecting from his father, except without the good humor.

Uncle Jonathan waved David into his enclosure. "Come on. I've got some good work for getting rid of frustration."

He'd do anything to postpone his arrival home. David glowered in the direction of his father's house and detoured into his uncle's gate.

Uncle Jonathan led him to the oxen stall on the ground floor of his house. "With the rain, things are getting too slippery in here. Load up the cart with the dung and add it to the pile in back."

His uncle patted him on the back and left him to it.

David picked up the pitchfork and attacked the dung and ground-in grasses. Every time he stuck the fork into the layer of waste on the floor, he got more worked up.

"It's not like I *wanted* to come back so soon. Nothing is ever my *choice*. The king decides. I wanted to stay. And if my *father* gets after me about it–" He barely paused to wipe the back of his grimy wrist across his eyes before any tears actually made their way out. "I'll do *nothing*, as usual. Not even when *Eliab* pushes me around. It's not my *place*."

He was still muttering when he wheeled out the second cartful.

"David!" Uncle Jonathan stood by the trough, holding up a jug. "Time for a water break."

David lifted his hand to indicate he heard. He couldn't let his uncle see him on the verge of crying over his father. Again. After he tipped out the cartload, he rubbed his bicep over his face to account for any redness. "Coming, uncle!"

When he put down the jug after gulping down his fill, his uncle dipped a rag into the jug and made like he was going to clean David's face. David reared out of range and cupped his hands into the trough and scrubbed the water over his skin. He refused to look at Uncle Jonathan's face. "There are a few more cartloads in there."

Uncle Jonathan grabbed his shoulder. "Let's go prep the dung for fuel first."

They squatted side by side, forming the dung and dried grasses into patties and tossing them aside to dry in the sun. David had twelve patties done when his uncle spoke.

"Where did the army go this time?"

"East. To Gad."

"Ammonites." Uncle Jonathan chuckled. "I'm surprised they had the courage."

"Who? Us or them?"

"Them, of course."

But it wasn't "of course." David glanced at his uncle while they worked. This was his best chance to ask, and his uncle the most likely person to answer. Everyone he asked at the fortress either changed the subject or hissed and made a sign for warding off evil.

He couldn't change the subject naturally, so he blurted out, "Did our army really run away from battle once?"

Uncle Jonathan sucked in a loud breath before snuffling his nose, clearing his throat, and spitting out a huge ball of fluid.

"I'll take that as a 'yes.'"

"How did you hear about that?"

His uncle kept working, so David did, too.

"The king told me."

"Our king? King Saul?"

David's neck prickled. "It's more like he talks to himself while I play. If I'm standing near him, I can hear some of it." He lobbed a finished patty onto the ground. "What about that battle?"

"You've heard the story hundreds of times."

David rested his forearms on his knees. "Only the part after Jonathan climbed that cliff. Nobody talks about what happened before."

"It's not a story for children."

"I'm not a child."

Uncle Jonathan sat back on his heels and seemed to stare through the dung pile. "I'd never seen an army like it. Thousands of chariots and horsemen. Their infantry covered the valley and the hills like they were grains of sand." He shivered. "I can see why those men took off."

"You didn't, though?"

His uncle shook his head.

"What about my father?" The words were out before David could take them back.

Uncle Jonathan smiled. "You should've seen him. He stood on a rock and rained curses down at the deserters. He bounded from cave to cave and made sure they knew what he thought of them."

David let go of the breath he'd been holding.

His uncle leaned close and whispered, "Even Maacah."

David gasped. "But he's an elder. He has the largest flock in all Bethlehem."

"The rich are not immune to fear."

"Why hasn't– Why didn't– How come–"

Luckily, his uncle knew what David couldn't bring himself to ask. "Why do you think the other elders defer to your father when he's mainly rich in–"

"Sons." David finished his father's favorite saying.

"Think about it."

David narrowed his eyes. "They can hardly bring themselves to look at him."

"Why?"

"They think they're better than us because they're richer."

But Uncle Jonathan was shaking his head. "What are other reasons a person will avoid eye contact? Think of your own life."

David came up with several without trying hard. You're lying. You're hiding. You're embarrassed. You're ashamed.

So all those times he'd seen Maacah and some of the other elders turn their faces from Jesse weren't because of their sense of superiority? "They aren't snobs?"

"They might be, but about this..."

"They're ashamed." David crumbled a handful of grasses. "They should be. The Lord gave them an overwhelming victory."

"How could they know that before it happened?"

"Because it's the Lord. He gives His people victory."

Uncle Jonathan fixed David with a patient look. "Yes, He does. But you didn't see what they saw. And you didn't live under the thumb of the Philistines for decades, nor the Egyptians for four hundred years. The Lord doesn't always immediately save."

David sputtered. His uncle was right, but he was also dead wrong.

His uncle put his hand up before David managed to get

any words out. "Did you want to hear the story or argue with me?"

"Story," David said right away.

Uncle Jonathan lifted an eyebrow.

"Please."

"When I and the other scouts–"

"You were a scout?"

Uncle Jonathan sighed.

"I'll glue my mouth shut," David said. "I swear."

"Less swearing, more doing. We saw the enormous Philistine encampment with all their iron weapons and armor glinting in the sun and sprinted back to tell Saul and Abner and then anyone else who would listen. Maybe we shouldn't have, but we couldn't see what we saw and then keep it inside. The next morning, hundreds of men had melted away like fat before the fire. And that happened every night until we were left with six hundred men." He shook his head. "Six hundred against those thousands."

"And the Lord."

Uncle Jonathan smirked. "Yes, six hundred men and the Lord."

"I would *never* have run away."

"No. I don't believe you would've."

"I will always trust Adonai to help me."

That wiped the indulgent look off his uncle's face. "That's a big thing you're saying."

If this had been a conversation with his father, David would have agreed and gone on his way. But if he couldn't say these things to Uncle Jonathan, he couldn't say them to anybody. "I know it with every part of me."

"Is this because of the anointing?"

David traced a nonsense design in the dirt. "In part."

"I want to know." Uncle Jonathan spoke quietly and seriously, which gave David the courage to go on.

"The anointing was one thing on one day, but He keeps–" He took a breath. "Keeps filling my heart."

His uncle looked like he was about to say something embarrassing, so David leapt in. "Back to the story?"

Uncle Jonathan nodded several times. "Men kept disappearing and Samuel kept not showing up, so Saul did the burnt offering and peace offerings himself before we went from Gilgal to Geba."

David couldn't stop himself from asking, "What about Samuel? Samuel came, didn't he?"

His uncle frowned like he was trying to remember and then raised his eyebrows. "Yes, he came as Saul was finishing up the sacrifices, spoke with the king, and left."

"What did he say?"

"Nobody was close enough to hear."

"What was the king like afterward?"

"I thought you were going to stop interrupting."

David drew out the word like a begging child would. "Please."

"I don't know. I don't recall anything in particular, so he must've been the way he always was."

David didn't listen as his uncle finished the story; he knew the rest. What he didn't know was what Samuel said to King Saul that made him so upset. The king always muttered at that point. No matter how close David got to the throne or how quietly he managed to play, he could never hear exactly what the king's complaint with the prophet and with Adonai was.

*****

Four moons later, late spring 1024 bce

Lately, Uncle Jonathan was full of stories about the Lord teaching His people to trust Him and wait patiently.

It was the most irritating lesson of all the lessons his uncle had tried to teach him over the years—made even worse because he was right. It took all the patience David could muster to endure day after day in the hills, watching the sheep, when he knew that King Saul and the entire army of Israel were fighting the Philistines yet again, this time within a day's journey.

He was tired of being sent back to Bethlehem. At first, it was fine to be home, to talk everything over with Joab, to do his duty to his father and the flock. But he'd just turned sixteen, and was as tall and strong as almost any man. The standing army was large enough that he didn't have to hide to practice with them anymore. He even knew military strategy from playing quietly enough in the receiving room to hear Abner and King Saul discuss it. He wasn't the same green fourteen-year-old who'd arrived at the fortress.

This must be how Joab felt all the time: actually aching to join the fighting.

But he couldn't. From his favorite high rock outcrop on the tallest hill outside Bethlehem, he took a stone out of his pack and loaded it into his sling's pouch.

"This one's for Abner," he shouted into the wind as he sent the stone far out on the other side of the hill.

Abner hadn't given him any chance to show what he could do. He'd dismissed David without looking him in the eye. "You're a boy and boys go home to their fathers," was all he said.

David humphed. He was as able to fight as any of his brothers. More so, because he'd been training for it while they'd been working the field.

He picked up his staff in his left arm and held his right arm up with the elbow bent and made like he was an armor bearer, protecting his master with his shield while striking the attackers. Sometimes, he could get the goats to charge him, but not today. It was too hot.

"And this one's for Eliab." David grunted as he heaved the next stone through some scrub.

There had been no need for Eliab to twist his ear in

front of Abner and the captains, and definitely no need for him to mock David until everyone laughed.

David emptied his bag and sent the next three stones in quick succession to the west, where he knew the army was. They could have made him a slinger.

What was taking them so long, anyway? He'd been in Bethlehem for forty-two days and there was no word about the battle. It was fully summer and hot as an oven. The wadis were mostly dried up. If he was having a hard time finding enough water for the sheep, how was Abner doing with thousands of soldiers?

Whatever was happening with the army, if they relied on Adonai, they'd win. Which was the problem. David knew Saul's feelings about that all too well.

He could have made a difference there, too. They could have let him come along and sing songs of encouragement to the soldiers. Like this one:

> Arise, Adonai, and scatter your enemies.
> Let those who hate you run for their lives.
> Drive them off like smoke in the wind.
> Melt them like wax in fire.
> The Lord announces victory.

The sheep chewed up at him, unimpressed.

"It's a good song," he told them. Especially the part about their enemies disappearing like smoke in the wind.

Out of the corner of his eye, he saw a streak of movement across a lower slope. He crouched and scanned the hills, his fingers scrabbling for rocks. Why did he already let all his big ones fly?

Soon, the culprit came into view. It was his nephew, Asahel, running full out. David jumped up and hollered.

Asahel was only slightly winded when he reached David, even though he'd run all the way from the village.

"What news?" David didn't have to say, "of the battle," because it was all he and his nephews could talk about.

"None," Asahel said. "But your father is sending food and you get to bring it."

David started for home, but a few steps in, doubled back. "You're staying with the flock, right?"

Asahel rolled his eyes and waved David on.

David didn't need any more encouragement. He was finally going to see battle.

9. Finally: battle

Jesse was in the storeroom at the back of the house when David slid to a stop in front of him. "I didn't mean come right now."

David was panting so hard he could barely hear. He bent over and put his hands on his knees, watching sweat plop onto the floor as he prayed that his father wouldn't change his mind.

"Since you're here." Jesse sighed. "Bring these out front."

David carted everything his father told him to, practically dancing in and out of the house.

"Do not get in the way of the soldiers or ask more questions than necessary to bring us news." Jesse frowned at David and then at the supplies. "This war's gone on long enough." He hefted one more bundle from the storeroom. "We can't send any more food. Your mother's already worried about *this*. The half-bushel of barley and ten loaves of bread should go to your brothers, and the ten cuts of pressed cheese to their captain."

David scooped it all up and headed for the gate.

"Stop!"

Half the food tumbled out of David's arms when he

halted. He knelt to pick up the items and spilled everything else. "Sorry, Father. I'll get it. It looks fi–"

"Calm down," Jesse said. "The Valley of Elah is more than a half day's walk and you've been in the hills all morning. I don't care how loudly you insist that no harm will come to you because the Lord is with you, you're not going out in the heat of the day for an errand that can wait until tomorrow."

David crouched among the scattered food. His thigh muscles twitched. Everything in him strained to go, but if his father said wait, then he had to wait.

It took several trips to stack the bundles inside the house. How would he carry it tomorrow? He poked around the storage area while his parents reconfigured the supplies remaining at home.

"In my day," Jesse said to Nitzevet, "we left the battlefield when our fathers needed us. How am I supposed to harvest and thresh all the wheat with three sons gone? I can't hold off much longer."

Nitzevet tut-tutted. "That's the price of having a king."

Jesse grunted. "We can't say Samuel didn't warn us."

"At least David was here to help with the lambing," Nitzevet said.

His father nodded.

When he couldn't stand his parents' silence anymore, David blurted, "Do I get a donkey to carry everything?"

Jesse shrugged. "Our neighbor sent his to the front last week and it never made it back."

That was fine, actually. Donkeys could carry a lot but they didn't always like to keep moving, and if he had one, he'd have to travel near water or carry water for the animal, either of which would slow him down.

"Come here." Jesse squatted on the floor and brushed a patch of dirt clear with the flat of his hand. When David was beside him, he drew a circle with his finger. "This is Bethlehem." Then he made a series of lines radiating south and west, ending in a valley between a few large hills. "This is the south road out of the village. Take it until you reach a dead sycomore tree." He moved his finger along the lines as he spoke. "Turn to the west there. Climb the hill until you're on a ridge above a dry streambed. That's the Wadi al-Nativ. Go along there until the land in front of you pitches down. Not to your right. Straight ahead. Do you hear me?"

"Yes, Father."

"Where do you go from here?" Jesse poked the ground hard enough to lift up a puff of dust.

David dug his thumbnail into the side of a finger to keep his answer respectful. "Straight ahead and down."

"No going your own way because you think you can figure out something better. That is the route we've always taken. That is the route you'll take. The forest is heavy there, oaks, but soon you'll be able to hear the armies."

"Are there any villages along the way?"

"None, and no springs nearby, so take all the water you'll need."

"How long?"

Jesse glanced at the pile of food packages. "Normally, half a day, but carrying those by yourself..."

"I can do it," David said quickly.

"Maybe your mother is right," Jesse said. "I should send one of your brothers with you."

David held his breath.

"Except that I can't spare anyone else."

"I can do it." At least this time David managed not to sound whiny. "Is there an extra yoke I could use?"

Nitzevet found one, but it needed new rope and they didn't have any to spare. She sent him to her brother Jonathan's.

Uncle Jonathan and his family were cleaning up after their midday meal. His uncle smiled when David bounded over. "This is a pleasant surprise."

"I'm on a mission." David bobbed on the balls of his feet. "Father is sending me to the front with some food and a letter for my brothers and I need a yoke to carry it all because there isn't a donkey and we don't have an extra rope so my mother–"

"Slow down." Uncle Jonathan laughed. "Slow down."

David's cheeks ached from grinning so widely. "Do you have any rope I could use to carry food to the army?"

His uncle nodded to his aunt and she went into the house. "So, you finally get to see the fight."

"I know. I can't believe it."

Uncle Jonathan raised an eyebrow. "What will your other master say when he sees you? He keeps sending you back here."

David craned his head to see whether his aunt had that rope yet. "There are thousands of men in the army. I won't even see the king."

"Probably true." Uncle Jonathan handed him a piece of bread. "So why didn't you hide in the ranks and tag along with them this time?"

David spoke while he chewed. "Father would know."

"How?"

"He knows the king always sends me home. Besides, the army passed through Bethlehem to gather men. I'd have had to lie to my father's face." David shuddered.

"So you told him about killing that bear last week?"

"That's different."

Uncle Jonathan looked at the air above David's head—his signal that he was waiting for David to answer the question more fully.

"That's...not telling everything."

Uncle Jonathan's smile was patronizing. "You know it's wrong, or you wouldn't skulk around here afterwards."

"If he didn't give me a lecture about not upstaging my brothers every time I kill a lion or a bear, I'd tell him."

His uncle put his right arm around David's shoulders. "You're a good boy." He pulled back and looked David over. "Young man. You're a good young man. Let's go see what your aunt has for you."

David let his uncle steer him to the house. "Why do you think the battle is taking so long?"

"Every battle is different. This one must be different in a new way."

David frowned. "That's not very helpful."

Uncle Jonathan shrugged. "I'm not there."

His aunt appeared in the doorway with a coil of rope. How much longer would he have to talk with his uncle? Would Uncle Jonathan be offended if David got what he came for and took off right now?

"David, listen to me. War is..."

Was his uncle ever going to finish that sentence? "War is what?"

"War is more and less than you could ever imagine."

David blinked. Those were his words of wisdom? "Thank you," he said, mostly so he could get out of there.

Uncle Jonathan sighed. "You're not listening. Go." He pushed David between the shoulder blades. "Have your adventure."

David nabbed the rope and ran backwards through their courtyard. "I'm going to hook it up right now."

Once home, David tied equal amounts of bread and cheese to either side of the yoke and fashioned a backpack out of the rope and the grain sacks. It balanced well enough for several steps, but after a full turn around the yard the wood gouged the soft parts of his shoulders and the rope chafed his skin raw.

That wasn't going to work.

He couldn't take a donkey, but maybe he could *be* the donkey. There had to be something without wheels he could pull on the ground. There was no spare wood, so the best he could hope for would be a sheep or goat skin big enough to wrap around everything, so the rough terrain wouldn't make things tumble out.

He found his mother pouring oil into the family lamps. She held up a finger and he waited until she was done.

David lowered his voice even though his father was in the fields. "The yoke isn't working. Do we have any skins I could use to make something to drag behind me?"

Nitzevet frowned. "Nothing big. Our last two whole sheepskins went with your brothers for their tent."

His eyes widened in a silent plea.

Her expression softened. "You know where the pile is. See if you can piece something together."

The pile of skins yielded five pieces he could sew together, including two largish thick ones that hadn't been completely scraped of fur that he could use for the bottom. He took three bone needles and several lengths of sinew and got to work.

It was a good thing his fingertips were so calloused

from playing his lyre. The amount of pressure it took to drive the bone through the tough, unstretched animal skin made his hands ache before he'd even gotten two pieces sewed together. But he kept at it. He'd prove to his father that it wasn't a mistake to send him to the front.

Once the whole thing was together he cut two holes in the front edge and attached rope to the side edges so he could close the skins around the food. He pushed Uncle Jonathan's rope through the holes and tied the ends around his chest and shoulders. Once the sled was loaded with the food tributes, he took it for a spin around the yard.

After two laps, the pressure of the rope around his front got to be too much, so he gathered the leads in his fist and created some slack. He grinned. This was going to work!

That night, he didn't sleep on the roof with the rest of his family. He was leaving as soon as the sun lightened the sky tomorrow, so to avoid waking anyone or tripping in the dark, he slept in the storage room next to his sled.

It took a long time for him to fall asleep. His thoughts kept whirling: tracing and retracing the path to the Valley of Elah, anticipating the sights of battle, wondering whether the Philistine army was as impressive as in the soldiers' stories. He tried to block out the last words of his father—"*You are delivering food, not joining the army. Do not draw attention to yourself in any way and do not pester the soldiers with your questions*"–but he worried the thought as if it were a bad tooth.

The house was thick with heat and there was no breeze to cool his skin, but he must have slept somehow. It was still dark when he opened his eyes. His breakfast was exactly where he'd left it the night before, in a covered bowl by his right hand. He carried the bowl outside and stared at the horizon, willing the sun to rise. There was a haze in the sky to the east, and the birds were singing, but there was no moon.

Soon, his food was eaten and his prayers said, and still there wasn't enough light to walk by. He went back in the house and strapped on his belt with his traveling lyre, his sling, and his filled water skin. He checked the knots on the sled for at least the seventh time. When he went outside, the haze in the sky had expanded. Below the range of blues was a pale strip the color of an apricot.

This was the sign he'd been waiting for. His feet scrambled on the gravel and he nearly fell, but he put his right hand on the ground, regained his footing, ran to the house, strapped on the sled and left.

Gentle laughter came from the roof. His mother stuck her head over the edge. "Haven't you left yet? What are you stalling for?"

David didn't react to her teasing beyond a wave. He grabbed his shepherd's staff and headed for his first landmark: the dead sycomore.

The journey took longer than he'd anticipated. He was slower. The food was heavier. The sled caught on rocks and tipped over a lot. Nothing spilled out and the skins didn't rip, but every time he'd have to stop, right it, rebalance the load so it wouldn't lurch again, and readjust the ropes before he could get going. By midday, his shoulders were blistered and his thigh muscles burned, but he pressed on. He had to get as far as he could by sunset, had to prove he was up to this and any task.

By dusk, he was an hour away from the battlefield, at most, but then the sled tipped and he didn't have the strength to resist its pull and was dragged downhill until he slammed into a tree. The air was knocked out of him. He couldn't die like this. His throat spasmed. Nobody would know where he was for days. Weeks would pass before they'd find his body. Wild animals would–

And then he took a successful breath.

But there would be no more progress that night.

David untied himself, drew his cloak over his body and curled up on the spot. He fell asleep in the middle of thanking Adonai for getting him this far.

In the morning, he stuffed the last of his food in his mouth, gulped the last of his water, and stared at the sled until the sun filtered through the trees.

He dragged the sled back to the crest of the hill and prepared himself to take on the burden, but when he looped one rope over his shoulder, his knees buckled from the pain. He pulled at the neck of his tunic. There were three angry red stripes, one by each shoulder and one around his chest.

No way could he bear the sled like he did yesterday.

So he'd pull the sled the way he brought it up the hill just now: walking backwards with the ropes in his hands. The crest didn't have any trees at the very top. As long as he kept the wadi crevice to his right, he'd be fine.

His back was on fire, but he could steer the sled better.

Then the hill sloped down and got heavily wooded, just like Father said it would. He had to turn sideways and send the sled in front of him, where its momentum could work to his advantage, for once.

It was hard to hear anything other than his own crashing through the woods, so he stopped now and then. The third time paid off. It was nothing distinct, distant voices and scuffling sounds, but enough to let him know he was getting close. He hurtled down the slope, not caring how many trees the sled bumped into or how many branches whipped against his face.

There was a break in the woods. What it revealed made him stop short. The Philistine army spread out over the opposite slope, the entire thing. The rising sun glared off all the Philistine bronze and iron. So much metal. And there were the enemy's chariots and horses, lined up, facing the Israelite camp. So far, Uncle Jonathan was right about one thing: it was more than he'd imagined.

But David wasn't discouraged. He sang under his breath,

> The best-equipped army cannot save a king.
> Great strength is not enough to save a warrior.
> Your warhorse won't give you victory.
> It might be strong, but it can't save you.
> We count on Adonai alone to save us.
> Only He can help us, protecting us like a shield.
> Our hope is in Him alone.

He rushed down the ridge, the pain in his back and shoulders gone. When he broke out of the forest, the Israelite soldiers were streaming out of their camp to the valley. They lifted their weapons and belted out a shrill battle cry.

Shivers broke out over his skin. This was it. He scanned the camp until he found what looked like a supply tent, dumped his gifts, slung his staff around his back, and sped after the soldiers. The Philistine army came down their hill, too, except they marched in rank, their coordinated footsteps rumbling like thunder.

And then everybody stopped. David backtracked so he could get high enough to see what was happening.

Each army stayed on the flats of their side of the valley. Each group had weapons in hand, but nothing was happening. Spears were being used as walking staffs and shorter weapons still hung from soldiers' belts. Nobody was even rustling or exhorting the men to continue. Not on either side. They were on the battlefield, but there was no battle. This was not what he'd expected.

David sidled up to the archers in the back. "What's going on?"

Their bows were armed, but the arrows pointed at the ground. "Same thing happens every day."

"Twice a day," said another man.

They didn't say anything else.

"You know where the division from Judah is?"

They pointed it out to him and he weaved through the crowd to find his brothers. If he had his way, he'd ask around some more before going to see them, but if Eliab found out he hadn't come to see them first, it would be one more example of his lack of respect and Eliab would make sure it got back to Father and he'd never be trusted with an important job again.

David waited until he was right behind them. "Abinadab. Shammah."

They glanced back and then did a double take, laughing and hugging him once they recognized him.

"What are you doing here?" Abinadab asked.

"Bringing you food and taking back news." David tried to seem casual. "Where's Eliab?"

Shammah said, "He's tall and imposing, so they put him up front."

David was man enough to admit to himself that he was

relieved Eliab wasn't nearby. It must have shown on his face, because his brothers smirked.

"Why did everyone stop?" David looked down and gasped. "And why are you still in sandals?"

Shammah said, "Huh?"

"You told me sandals get too slick with blood during a battle, so you fight barefoot." David pointed at all the feet around them. "Sandals. Everyone."

Abinadab gestured to the front with his chin. "You'll see soon enough."

"You wouldn't believe it if we told you," Shammah said.

David scowled. "Would, too. I'm not a child."

A sound like sheep make when they're panicked rose from the front of the line.

"I can't see," David said.

His brothers bent their knees and each slapped a thigh, making a stool for him, so David put his right hand on Abinadab's shoulder and his left on Shammah's, planted his feet on their legs, and hoisted himself up.

They were right. He wouldn't have believed it.

10. It is you

In front of the Philistine ranks was the most massive human being David had ever seen. Tall as the tallest tree in the family compound, he wore a bronze helmet and a skirt of little pieces of bronze. The bronze on his chest armor was patterned like two mountains meeting in a deep valley. Even his legs were protected by bronze leggings. There was as much bronze on him as on five of the wealthiest Israelite soldiers.

And his spear...David had never seen anything so terrifying. Its shaft was the size of a weaver's beam and the spearhead was iron. There was a bronze javelin slung over his back and a straight sword as tall as David hanging off his belt. His armor bearer struggled with a shield that was three times as wide as his own body.

This giant planted himself between the two armies. His laughter made David's skin crawl. The giant's voice was deep and guttural, as if it had a hard time making its way out of that enormous body. "Here you are, the army of Israel. Do you need a whole army to settle this? Choose someone to fight for you, and *I'll* represent *my* people. We'll settle this dispute in a single combat!"

Shammah told David, "Same thing every day, twice a day, for the past forty days."

"Interrupting morning and evening prayers," Abinadab said.

David goggled at the giant. "*That's* why the battle's taking so long."

"If your man is able to kill me, then we will be your slaves." The giant glanced back at his army, and they slapped their legs and acted like that was the most hilarious thing they'd ever heard.

David craned his head around to see whether anyone was preparing to step forward, but the Israelites shrank back even more.

"But if I kill him," the giant continued, "you will be our slaves." He lumbered a few massive steps closer. "I defy the armies of Israel! Send me a man who will fight with me! Prove to me my grandmother didn't make up your god to scare me."

David went very still.

This was what an enemy was. He thought he'd understood it before, but acting out war with Joab, learning about military strategy, seeing soldiers between battles and hearing their stories—none of that prepared him for the malicious intent, the lack of respect this enemy had. Fighting wasn't only about glory. It was equally about defending the honor of the Lord and Israel's dependence on Him.

He'd never heard anyone mock Adonai. Cry out to Him,

ask where He was, plead with Him for help—he'd heard all those. But this was jeering, this was ridicule.

How could the men of Israel stand by? The giant issued a direct challenge that had remained unmet, day after day after day. No wonder he thought Israel's God was worthless and powerless.

A soldier nearby held his hand out, palm down. It trembled like an old man's.

David climbed down from his perch on his brothers' knees. "How long does he talk for?"

Shammah was brushing sand from his leg, so Abinadab answered. "Sometimes an hour, sometimes he gets bored after ten minutes."

"And nobody has met his challenge?"

His brothers shook their heads.

"Why not?"

"You've seen him," Abinadab said. "His left leg is bigger than your whole body."

David's eyes stung from holding them so round. "There has to be one man who trusts that the Lord will give him victory."

"Our army versus their army, absolutely," Shammah said. "But man to man with *that* man...."

Abinadab put a heavy hand on David's shoulder. "Nobody wants to be the one who sends us back into slavery."

"So we send him one man at a time, but close together,

like when little birds pester a hawk into leaving them alone. Or send an archer to kill him from a distance."

"Their army will be waiting," Abinadab said.

David let his exasperation get the best of him. "We trick the Philistines all the time, climbing up to their lines at night, sneaking up and attacking them from the rear. Why is this different?"

Shammah's hand fell on David's other shoulder. "If we send even one man out there, we agree to his terms."

David shrugged off his brothers and took off blindly.

Even growing up with all the stories about Adonai doing unbelievable things—parting the Red Sea, the pillar of fire and of cloud in the desert, manna on the ground, the walls of Jericho, victory after victory—nobody in the entire army would step forward? Nobody?!

Somebody needed to remind them who they were.

Not even his own father could object to that, since, according to Uncle Jonathan, Jesse had done the same thing to his comrades when he'd been a soldier.

David stopped and asked the nearest soldier, "Who is this pagan Philistine anyway?"

"Goliath of Gath." The soldier's gaze was trained on the giant.

"Why are we letting him defy the armies of the living God?"

"Look at him."

"Why haven't you met his challenge?"

“Like I said, look at him.” The soldier sounded so resigned.

“But the Lord will give you the strength and the cunning.” David poured all his confidence in Adonai into his words. “He will give you the victory. I know He will.”

The soldier ruffled his hair as if his words were the adorable babbling of a toddler. It was infuriating. David tried this with two other soldiers with the same result. A fourth soldier said that the reward was tempting, but he wasn’t good enough at hand-to-hand.

So David moved on and asked a fifth soldier, “What will a man get for killing this Philistine and putting an end to his abuse of Israel?”

The soldier sighed. “The king will give him one of his daughters for a wife and his whole family won’t have to pay taxes. Every night, I decide it’ll be me, but then every morning good sense returns.”

After that exchange, David wound through the ranks, looking for men whose armor was made of stiffened wool. Maybe an appeal to their family’s poverty would be more convincing than a call to trust Adonai. “Is it true that King Saul will make you his son-in-law and your whole family, your father and all your siblings, won’t have to pay taxes ever again?”

The answer was always a variation on, “Yes, we’ve heard, and yes, we’re tempted,” but they’d watch Goliath wave his spear, and then shudder and turn away.

He'd only talked to a few poorer soldiers when he was hauled backwards by his ear until he fell.

Eliab loomed over him. "What are you doing here?" He jabbed David with the toe of his sandal, hitting David's chest right where the rope burn was.

David curled his arm around his middle and scooted back on his behind, grinding grit into his skin.

"What about those sheep you're supposed to take such good care of?"

"Father sent me here with food for you and gifts for your captain." David scrambled to his feet and moved farther away. "And to bring back news."

Eliab curled his lip. "A fine excuse. As if you hadn't been hounding him for weeks. I know all about your pride and dishonesty. You just want to see the battle."

The soldiers around them laughed. Eliab's accusation might be partly true, but it was also unjust. David's skin burned.

"You've delivered your food and now you've seen the giant." Eliab pointed to the east. "Go back home where you belong."

"You should be ashamed by the news I'm going to deliver."

Eliab's face looked as hard as flint. "What was that?"

The surrounding soldiers backed up a few steps, forming a circle around them.

"What will Father say when I tell him that nobody will

be back in time for the wheat harvest because you're all too afraid to fight one man?" As soon as the words were out of his mouth, he knew he'd gone too far.

Eliab's skin turned purple.

David edged one foot backwards and Eliab lunged at him. There was no question of standing his ground. Eliab was taller and stronger and meaner, so David used his speed and smaller size to squeeze through the circle of soldiers, pushing aside spears and dodging axes until he couldn't hear his brother crashing and cursing behind him. He was checking over his shoulder when he ran into something solid.

Abinadab's chest.

"There you are." Abinadab put his arm around David. "Look, I remember being fifteen."

"Sixteen," he corrected between heaving breaths.

Abinadab did a bad job of hiding his patronizing smile. "Even worse, then. You've got all your high ideals, but that's because reality hasn't beaten them down yet."

David twisted free and crossed his arms.

"We've all seen battle." Abinadab gestured at the men around them. "We've seen our comrades' heads caved in, and we know how little it takes to crack open a skull. We've seen a spear go through a friend's body to stick out the other side, and we've wound up with hands drenched in the blood of our enemies from doing the same. You see these big, strong bodies and wonder why they don't fight the giant. We see fragile piles of skin and flesh and blood, so much blood, so easily spilled. Israel's strength has always been together, not alone."

Our strength is in the name of Adonai, who made heaven and earth.

That's what David wanted to say, but nobody was responding to that, so David gave his brother a more historical argument. "What about Jonathan? He took on twenty Philistines with only a sword and his armor bearer. And Shamgar, the judge who killed six hundred Philistines with an ox goad? And–"

Abinadab looked alarmed. "Turn around and bow and don't say a word." He lowered his own head.

David glanced behind him and saw Abner approaching. He did as his brother ordered. Soon, he saw feet with dirty sandals and leather straps circling thick legs, the calf muscles jutting out like jar handles.

"Are you the one pestering the soldiers about the giant?" Abner's voice was weary, not at all how he sounded back at the compound.

David knew better than to object to the accusation of pestering. "Yes, my lord."

Abner seized David's upper arm, his fingertips digging in. David's knee-jerk reaction was to clench his fist and harden his muscle.

Abner snorted. "The king wants to see you." He pulled David alongside him.

"My lord." Abinadab spoke from behind them. "He's my brother."

"You had your chance to rein him in earlier," Abner said.

"My father would want me to accompany him."

"The king means him no harm."

David snuck a peek. The commander's face didn't look reassuring.

"Sir, he's my youngest brother. My duty—"

Abner raised his free hand. "Fine. But be quiet."

Every several steps, Abner yanked on David's arm as if he weren't keeping up, even though he was. It was a useless show of domination. Wouldn't the army be better served by manhandling the enemy rather than a sixteen-year-old?

It is you.

David frowned and looked around. Abner was staring straight ahead and not acting like he'd said anything. That wasn't his brother's voice, either. Nobody else was close enough to him to have spoken that quietly and clearly.

Even though that voice didn't belong to anyone he could see, and it didn't speak again, somehow, with every step, David shed his dread and his defiance like a snake shedding its skin.

He recognized this feeling.

It was the same as when he lay on his back at night and

sang about the glory of the heavens. It was the same as when he'd cradled that lamb in his arms after he saved it from the lion's jaws.

This feeling meant that the Spirit of the Almighty was with him.

What seemed impossible a few heartbeats ago was now the only reasonable course of action.

So when Abner brought him to a halt in front of King Saul, he didn't wait for the king to speak first. "Don't worry about a thing. I'll fight this Philistine."

David waited through the stunned silence of the men around him.

"Do not be ridiculous." Saul's eyebrows formed a dark line across his forehead. "You are a boy, and he has been in the army since he *was* a boy!"

Abinadab whispered David's name. His eyes were shut and he held out his right hand, as if asking David to come with him and not bother these people anymore. King Saul was already turning away.

"I've been taking care of my father's sheep for years." David wanted the ground to open up and swallow him. Why couldn't the Spirit of Adonai prevent his voice from cracking, now of all times?

"A shepherd boy?" Saul mocked his breaking voice. "A shepherd boy is going to volunteer when none of my trained warriors will? Is this a joke? Because it isn't funny."

David spoke with calm and serious purpose. "When a

lion or a bear comes to steal a lamb from the flock, I go after it and take the lamb from its mouth. If the animal turns on me, I catch it by the jaw and club it to death. I've done this to lions and bears, and I'll do it to this Philistine, too." His hands clenched into fists. "The Lord who saved me from the claws of the lion and the bear will save me from this giant."

"Idle boasting," Saul said.

How could the king be so dismissive? Hadn't those three years of faithful service taught him anything about David and what he could do with Adonai's blessing?

"My lord." Abinadab's voice was thin. "May I speak?"

Down came Saul's eyebrows again. "Who are you?"

"I am his brother, my lord. And what he says is true." Abinadab swallowed audibly. "He's not exaggerating about the lions and bears."

Saul stepped away and tilted his head for Abner to follow. They didn't bother to keep their voices down.

"It's a suicide mission," Saul said.

"Nobody else is going to do it," Abner said. "The men are scared and bored, and we're out of food. I don't know how much longer the army will hold together."

Saul squeezed his temples. "It's embarrassing. I should order you to do it."

Abner coughed. "I'm too old to think I'm invincible and too valuable to you to be thrown away like that."

"I know." Saul frowned at the ground. "Should I compensate his father for the child dying so cruelly?"

Abinadab put his hand on David's shoulder. Whether it was to comfort him or encourage him despite the king's words, David didn't care. He shook off his brother. He wasn't sad or frightened. He wanted to jump up and down and yell at them to be ashamed for having so little faith.

Abner shrugged. "His brother is here. He'll confirm that the boy volunteered and we rejected his offer but the boy insisted."

"There's still the problem of the giant's terms," Saul said. "The boy will lose and we'll be slaves."

Saul and Abner stared at Goliath for the rest of their conversation.

Abner stroked his beard. "We're sending a *boy*, not a *man*, which isn't exactly agreeing to the giant's terms."

Saul hummed. "It will be hard to watch someone so young go to his death."

"It might be the best thing at this point. His martyrdom will enrage our men and we'll rout the Philistines when they come for us, thinking they'll enslave us. Their champion wins but their army loses."

"So we back into the hills and let them start looting our camp, and then we rush in and fight them on our ground, when they don't expect it?"

Abner nodded.

Saul tilted his head back and forth. "I like that." He drew himself up to his full height and faced David. "Go ahead."

David didn't care what they thought would happen or what plans they made. Adonai would come through for him. He bobbed his head once and turned away to march toward Goliath.

11. A single stone

David made it three steps before the king and Abner were yelling at him to stop. What did they want now?

Saul backhanded the shoulder of a man next to him. "He needs armor. If the boy is going to face the giant on behalf of all Israel, he needs the best." The king began to remove his own gear. "Help me, you fool!"

The armor bearer had been standing beside the king, a stunned look on his face, but then he jumped and got busy unhooking and untying. He told David to strip down to his loincloth.

David put his staff down, and then his pack on top of that. When he pulled his tunic over his head, there was laughter. Mocking laughter. There was nothing wrong with him. He wasn't a grown man, but he wasn't sickly looking, either, except maybe in comparison to Goliath.

Some soldiers were glancing at him and whispering to each other. Then he remembered about the rope burn.

David closed his eyes. *Don't think about that. Don't think about the fact that I'm standing in front of hundreds of men in only my loincloth. Focus on how Adonai will bless this fight.*

When he opened his eyes, the armor bearer was holding the king's breastplate up to him. It reached halfway down to David's knees.

David met the man's gaze. They both knew this was impossible.

"Put it on him, already," Saul said.

The armor bearer went to work, tying on the leg guards and fastening the breastplate around David's torso. The metal scraped his already raw skin. He clenched his jaw to keep from grimacing.

The skirt of mail slunk to the ground twice because the armor bearer couldn't cinch the waistband tightly enough. When David tried to step out of it, the tops of the shin guards bumped against the bottom of the breastplate and he had to hop to stay upright. He whispered to the armor bearer, "Not working."

"Just do it." The armor bearer strapped guards around David's shoulders and upper arms.

The armor was heavy, but that wasn't the real problem. The edges kept catching on each other, so he couldn't lift his arms higher than his waist.

Now the armor bearer was holding up the king's bronze helmet. David groaned, "Come on," but the man put it on his head, where it sank low enough to completely block his vision.

The strap for the king's sword had the same problem as the mail skirt. The sword dropped point down and canted off to the side. It would've sliced David's leg, except that there was no skin visible.

"See, it's working already," Abner said.

David didn't have to see the commander to know he was being mocked. He hiked up the helmet a bit. He felt like a little boy playing dress-up.

"Humor him," the armor bearer whispered and pressed the hilt of the king's sword into David's right palm.

David took a few experimental steps and stayed upright, but when he clasped the sword and swung it, he became totally unbalanced and lurched to the side. Only the quick actions of the armor bearer saved him from winding up in the dirt. The men around him muffled their snickers, but David could hear them.

For the first time since he offered to fight, he felt like a child.

He removed the helmet and shook his hair. "I can't go in these."

"These are the highest quality protections available. My own armor, still warm from my own back."

An offended King Saul was a dangerous King Saul, but there was no getting around the fact that this armor made David a joke, not to mention unable to move.

His heart knocked against the breastplate. "This offer from Adonai's Anointed is an honor too great for me. Unfortunately, the king himself is literally too great for me –" he risked a shaky smile–"and I'm not used to this glory. Please, my lord."

"Fine." The king gave a jerky wave. "Do it your way."

It was short work for David to wriggle out of the armor and into his tunic, hiking up and tying the hem so he could move. His shoulders unclenched when he had his own pack around his waist and his own staff in his hand.

The armor bearer nodded. "Whatever you're going to do, do it before you get in range of the giant's spear."

Saul made a big show of kissing him once on each cheek and announcing loudly, "May the Lord be with you." Then he muttered, "*He's* certainly not with me anymore."

David didn't think he was supposed to hear that, and he didn't know how to respond without his lyre in his hand, so he took a deep breath and headed out.

The soldiers around them opened up a path and someone yelled, "Out of the way for the giant killer."

David moved through a chaotic gauntlet of jeers, encouragement, expressions of disbelief. "We're doomed." "You've got to be kidding."

They were pressing in, closing ranks around him, jostling him and breathing on him. He leaned into the crowd, but couldn't make any headway. "Let me through." He pushed at them. "I need to get through." But it was like yelling into the wind.

Every time he made it a few steps, he'd get swallowed up again. He struggled to lift his staff in front of him and finally did it, clipping at least two soldiers in the chin. He was making a little more progress, but at this rate, it'd take him all morning to reach the front. For all he knew, Goliath was done and David had already lost his chance.

There was a commotion behind him, but he didn't turn around. He had to keep moving forward.

"What are you idiots doing? Give the boy some room," Abner bellowed behind him. The crowd eased and Abner and Abinadab were beside him, and then in front of him, clearing the way.

Suddenly, there was nobody to pass. He was there.

The two armies were close enough that David's seven-year-old niece could have hit the enemy with a rock from her sling. Why hadn't the Israelites just let their arrows and rocks fly from the rear and let the fight start in chaos without sending out a man?

Goliath was at the far end of the Israelite front line with his back to David. "I'm getting bored," he shouted. "Maybe I should choose my own challenger. Someone from here." He lunged toward the army. "Or here."

Wherever he aimed his body, the Israelite soldiers faded away and shifted like a flock of birds in the sky.

David walked steadily in the giant's direction, noting that the giant didn't move much from where he stood, and when he did more than lunge, he was slower than an old bear.

There was barely enough water left in the brook to

wet the bottoms of his sandals. He bent down and chose five beautiful stones: round and smooth and heavy. They knocked against each other in his bag as he advanced.

The giant was still toying with the Israelite army, but his comrades noticed David. They slapped their thighs and pointed and called out to Goliath.

"Finally!" Goliath shifted to a throwing grip on his javelin. The armor bearer turned him to face David. And then he laughed. He doubled over and laughed.

David kept walking.

When Goliath straightened, David got a good look at him. It was like different parts of his face had grown at different rates. His jaw was enormous, but his eyes seemed compressed by a forehead so massive that his helmet barely came down it halfway. In their training sessions, Jonathan had told him that archers and slingers aimed for the face. It had to be a blessing that this enemy had so much face to aim at.

The giant lifted his top lip in a sneer. "Am I a dog that you come at me with a stick! It offends Baal that Israel sends me a boy. Come over here, little boy, and I'll give your flesh to the birds. There isn't even enough of you to satisfy a lion!"

It didn't even register that David should be afraid.

He kept walking.

As "just David," he was a youngest son, a shepherd of a

small flock, a musician, a servant who did as he was told. As that boy, he didn't stand a chance.

But David plus Adonai was a different matter.

This must be what Samuel had anointed him to do. The Spirit of Adonai filled him with an odd peace as he headed for that armored tree of a man. It was like He had already won this battle and all David had to do was follow.

He lifted his head and looked the Philistine in the eye, never wavering the entire time he shouted, "You come at me with sword, spear, and javelin, but I come to you in the name of Adonai Almighty, the God of the armies of Israel. Today the Lord will conquer you, and I will kill you and cut off your head."

The giant replied, but David wasn't listening.

David's words weren't mere threats or boyish bravado; they were a promise. The power of Adonai coursed through him. "And then *we* will give the dead bodies of your men to the birds and wild animals, and the whole world will know that there is a God in Israel!" He raised his staff and then threw it on the ground. "Everyone will know that He doesn't need fancy weapons to rescue His people. It's His battle, not ours."

Goliath pointed his spear at David and took two steps while David ran right at him. David didn't need to slow or look down to perform movements he'd done hundreds of times: he reached into his bag and took out one of those perfect stones, nestled it into his sling, swung it one revolution at his side, and hurled it.

It hit the giant so quickly and so precisely in the middle of his forehead that he didn't even have time to look surprised before he fell on his face.

His armor bearer was as stiff as a wooden idol, staring open-mouthed at his boss. Dust was still billowing when David reached the giant unopposed, unsheathed Goliath's sword, and climbed onto his back, which raised and lowered with shallow breaths. He was still alive.

David braced himself with one foot on the ground and one foot on the giant's back, lifted the sword above his head as if it were no heavier than his shepherd's staff and swung down. He hit the exposed skin at the back of the giant's neck, sawing until he got all the way through the flesh and the bone.

It took several kicks at the base of the bronze helmet until it rolled away. With both hands, he grabbed the giant's head by the hair and hefted it as high as he could, displaying it first to the Israelite army, and then to the Philistine army.

All he could hear was the pounding of his blood in his ears and the huff of his own breathing. He'd done it. Adonai *had* given him the strength—although that seemed to be waning now that the deed was done. His arms were quaking.

Two roars sounded, one low and triumphant from the

Israelites and the other high and rising higher from the Philistine side.

David dropped the giant's head and let the Israelites stream around him on their way across the valley while he closed his eyes and offered his thanks. "You let me look down in triumph on my enemy. Praise the name of Adonai."

He opened his eyes and watched the developing battle. Should he join? He'd killed the giant, but he was a few years from military service age. Would that matter? What would his father say?

At the thought of Jesse, the meager contents of his stomach churned: he hadn't meant to, but he'd wound up drawing the most attention to himself possible.

Someone ran up from behind, hoisted him in the air, and jumped up and down several times before putting him back on his feet. It was Abner, who looked at him funny. "Hey? Aren't you the king's musical servant who asked to join the fight?"

David stumbled as he regained his footing. "Yes, my lo–"

"Joke's on me for saying no." Abner grinned and clapped his hands against David's shoulders. "The giant never saw it coming. Find a weapon and join in the fun. The enemy cannot win today!" He took off after the Philistines, laughing the whole way.

The giant's spear handle was so thick that David

couldn't get his hand all the way around. He picked up the sword and his arms shook hard enough that he had to drop it. How had he swung this over his head? He raised the javelin above his shoulder, but it was balanced for a much, much larger man, and he couldn't control it. Hopefully, when he got to the Philistine camp, there would be dropped clubs or axes he could snatch.

Until then, his sling had been good enough for the giant, so it'd be good enough for the man's comrades. David threaded the leads through his fingers and—

"Wait! Wait!"

It was the king and Jonathan and their armor bearers. By the time they reached him, he was shivering like he did when his mother put a wet tunic on him to cool down a burning fever.

"It's a proud day to be an Israelite," Saul said.

"That was amazing," Jonathan said.

David ducked his head into a bow. His teeth were chattering hard enough that he didn't want to speak.

"Who is your father? I need to congratulate him," Saul said.

Jonathan hung his head.

David almost blurted out, *Don't tell my father*, but managed to say, "J-J-Jesse of Bethlehem."

Saul frowned slightly. "That sounds familiar."

Did the king really not recognize him without his lyre in hand?

Jonathan whispered in his father's ear.

Saul blinked a little too often. "You've served your king well for years already. It will be even more so now. Your bravery has charged up my troops more than any prayer of Samuel's ever did!"

The Israelites running into battle were making so much noise that David wasn't sure he'd heard the king right. It wasn't his own bravery. "I can do anything through the Lord, who strengthens me."

"Of course. If Jonathan is my right hand, you will be my armor bearer, my shield, fighting at my other side." Saul turned to the man who'd tried to outfit David in the king's gear. "Join the infantry today. Hurry up, give him my shield so we can get in on the action."

David's mouth opened, but no sound came out.

The armor bearer pressed the bronze oval into David's hands. "I'm honored to pass the king's shield to the giant slayer."

The shield wasn't huge, but David shook so hard, it took both his hands to hold it steady.

"Put it on your right arm," Saul said. "Opposite from the regular soldiers."

"I know, my lord," David said. "I've been practicing."

Jonathan was holding something in the flat of his palms. "Take my sword. It's yours now."

"I couldn't–"

"You must." The sheath was attached to Jonathan's belt, so David got that, too.

Jonathan leaned close to cinch the belt around David's waist. "Don't worry. It'll get better."

"My lord?"

"The cold, the trembling."

David pulled back and gaped. How did he know?

"I practically shook myself out of my loincloth after that battle at Micmash. Speaking of which..." Jonathan handed David a soft brown bundle.

It was a short battle tunic.

"You're a real soldier now." Jonathan gave David a pointed look that didn't ease until David put it on over his own tunic and re-strapped the belt.

Saul gave a deafening battle cry and they ran past the deserted Philistine camp to Gath.

Jonathan was right. Warmth and strength returned to David's limbs the more he used them.

Real battle was so different from playing war games with his nephews. A sickly sweet and metallic scent hung in the air. His shoes were already slick from the blood on the ground, but the king kept moving and David didn't have time to take off his sandals. The thuds and crunches of clubs hitting bodies and the clangs of metal meeting metal were as thrilling as he'd imagined they would be, but they were mingled with the cries of the wounded and dying, which were real. He kept looking around for his brothers. Were any of those cries theirs?

Now that the surge from Adonai had ebbed, would he have the strength to kill a grown man? Would the king regret giving such an important job to someone so young?

They were fast approaching the fighting.

Please, Adonai, don't let me be the cause of the death of the king. Whatever happens to me, at least let Your Anointed One live.

12. Someone else, someone better

Saul had talked too long to the giant slayer. By the time the boy was ready, the rest of the army was way ahead of them, chasing down the Philistines and winning this war. The king wasn't supposed to be the clean-up crew, but now that he was, he'd make sure no Philistine who'd fallen could get up to fight again.

They strode along the road to Gath, and when they spotted a Philistine moving, skewered him where he lay. The boy watched Jonathan's armor bearer and learned quickly. He was so consistent about letting the king go in for the kill first that it got on Saul's nerves. "You're not a soldier until blood drips off your own sword." He gestured to the man struggling at their feet. "You take this one."

David stepped on the man's head and slit his throat.

Jonathan grinned. "You're getting a signature move."

Saul heard a thud behind him, and by the time he turned around, David was already there, blocking him with the shield. Two Philistine soldiers had used their dead comrades as cover and flung the bodies off before attacking.

David was aggressive with the shield, pushing it at the

enemy, lunging at them with his sword. Saul had room to get ready and time to plan his move. Counting Jonathan and his armor bearer, it was four against four. All of them had long, straight iron swords, so the enemy didn't have the advantage there. Saul needed to gain an edge.

"You know who that is?" Saul pointed his elbow at David. "He killed your giant and now he's coming for you!"

The whites of their eyes showed, like a donkey that spots a bee on its nose.

"Your giant was easier to kill than a salamander. You think your chariots and your iron make you invincible, but they don't!"

David's taunts distracted them long enough for Saul to move his head slightly to indicate the attack plan. He and Jonathan and the other armor bearer came at the Philistines from the sides, David took care of the one nearest him, and it was over before it began.

Saul had never been so in tune with an armor bearer. This David boy knew how to both protect his king and lash out at the enemy. The Philistines were falling as if this were a training exercise, not a battle against their most formidable foe.

With David at his side, Saul's legs were young again. He even ran into the hills after Philistines who tried to escape their sure fate. His shoulder moved freely again.

By the time they reached the base of Gath's hill, the gates were closed. A few Philistine soldiers climbed up the walls on ropes tossed over by their comrades inside the city: perfect targets.

Saul stayed out of range of the enemy archers on top of the wall, but the boy should have his fun. David. David should have his fun. It was so hard to think of him by his name after so many years of avoiding it. "Do you still have your sling?"

David checked his pack. "Yes, my lord."

"Go ahead."

David babbled his thanks. He bent to put Saul's shield on the ground, then looked for someone else to hold it, then clutched it to his chest.

After the boy's fierceness on the battlefield, it was endearing to see that he was still green. "I can hold my own shield."

The boy bowed his head and handed Saul the shield before taking off. He charged up beside the road, using the oaks for cover and then joined the other Israelite soldiers in darting out from behind trees and firing at the Philistines on the wall. Saul and the infantrymen set off huge cheers whenever the archers and slingers picked one off.

Abner came to stand beside Saul. The Philistine blood on his arms and breastplate was already drying and turning dark. "It's a good day to be an Israelite."

Saul lifted his sword high as another Philistine tumbled

to the dirt. "Where did my musician learn to fight like that?"

"He's been hanging around the edges of the army while we trained."

"Why didn't you tell me that earlier?"

"Lots of boys do," Abner said. "I don't pay attention to them. One of my officers had to tell me."

Saul sighed. "It'll be good to get home. A low-casualty routing of the enemy, not to mention the giant, should make it easier to get more soldiers to sign on next time."

"True, true." Abner sidled closer. "Our young friend vowed that the birds and wild animals would feast on the bodies of our enemies. And we take our vows seriously."

"We don't know anything about sieges." Saul sheathed his sword. "That's not the Israelite way."

Abner lowered his voice more. "Just long enough for animals to mutilate the carcasses."

"Not a true siege?"

Abner shook his head. "We'd position some men here and some halfway down the road to the battlefield so the Philistines can't sneak around the back way. The rest of us would stay near the enemy camp."

"To keep people from retrieving the bodies."

"That's all." Abner held up two fingers. "Maximum."

"Do we have enough food for two days?"

"We don't, but add the supplies from their camp and we'll get by."

Saul tapped his fingers against his biceps.

"We could thoroughly loot the camp," Abner said.

"And send a strong message to King Achish." Saul glared at the enormous double doors of Gath's gate. "He will think twice before invading our villages again."

"I don't know about that," Abner said. "With our land, they'd control the north-south and the east-west trade routes."

"They have the sea," Saul muttered. "Why can't they leave us to our own lives?"

The action at the walls was over and men were making their way down the hill, laughing and recounting the best of their kills.

"Let's do it," Saul said.

Abner tipped back his head and yelled, "Seven cheers for our warrior king!"

Saul let himself be hoisted onto several shoulders and marched down the road to their seven huzzahs. And then someone else called for the same for David, who soon appeared at Saul's level.

When those cheers died down, Saul raised his voice, repeating, "Men of Israel," until they were paying attention. "Men of Israel, the Lord was with us today!"

The soldiers got riled up again; Saul waited for quiet.

"David," he called out. "What did you say to that Philistine cur?"

David opened his mouth and took a deep breath, but

then he shook his head. "The Spirit of the Lord was speaking through me. I don't remember."

Saul smiled. "He said, 'we'll give the dead bodies of your men to the birds and wild animals, and the whole world will know that there is a God in Israel!'"

Everyone cheered wildly, bobbling Saul enough that he had to grip handfuls of the men's hair to keep his seat on their shoulders. This celebration was getting undignified, but he didn't have to hang on for much longer before he handed it over to Abner.

"Men of Israel," Saul cried. "Here, in your presence, I throw my full weight behind that vow. The Philistines will not be allowed to gather their dead for two days. In the daylight, we gather our plunder. At night, we guard the road until the dogs and vultures have done their dirty business with our enemies."

They put him down and he straightened his armor and buffed his armlets of office until they shone. Despite the hubbub, David was at his side before Saul could order someone to fetch him.

Saul slapped his back. "It's like you were born to be a soldier."

"Thank you, my lord. I won't let you down."

"Make a path for me. There's looting to do." Saul tossed his shield.

David caught it and darted in front of Saul. "Make way for Adonai's Anointed! Make way for Adonai's Anointed!"

It was a long way to the initial battlefield, and soon Saul felt every one of his fifty-eight years. The left knee that took a club three years ago twinged with every step; he adopted a statelier pace to avoid limping.

When they got there, some of the men were already going through the Philistine camp, making piles of weapons and silver and food, but even more men stood in a ring in the middle of the valley. The giant.

Even from a distance, Saul could see the forceful hand gestures and hear the arguing. He sighed and told David to lead him there. As soon as the men on the outside of the ring saw the high plume on his helmet, they quieted. Silence ran in a ripple toward the center.

"What's the problem here?" Saul was tired.

"I think this armor should go to our lord, the king, and they think it should be shared," someone said, setting off more shouting.

Saul stepped through the men to stand by the giant and raised his left hand. His right shoulder had stiffened up enough that he didn't think it would let his arm go that high. "Silence. Which of you had the courage to come out against him?" He kicked the giant's foot.

"That's right," Saul sneered. "None of you." He looked around the circle until the men had to feel properly ashamed that a boy did what they wouldn't do. "The spoils go to him. Bring the giant's gear and his head to the armor bearer's tent for David and feel lucky that I'm letting you take any plunder at all."

Saul and David were headed to the Philistine camp when Jonathan ran up. "Someone has spotted Philistine soldiers in the hills to the east. Who wants to chase them down with me?"

David was practically bouncing on his toes, but he had enough sense of his place not to ask to go. Saul sent him off just as much to reward him as to be rid of him and this youthful enthusiasm.

That night, while they ate their meager evening meal, no matter which group he visited, all Saul heard were stories about David's exploits. About how he spotted a hiding Philistine and flushed him out with his sling. About how like a goat he was, scrambling over hills and climbing hand over hand up rock faces. About how fearless he was. Each time, Saul's response was the same: "The Lord brought him to us just in time."

He retired to his tent early.

Two days later, on the way back to Gibeah with the conquering army, Saul wasn't on a chariot or even on a donkey. Trudging between Jonathan and David seemed like a good idea when Abner suggested it, but two hours into the march, Saul didn't care as much about making sure people connected him with Israel's newest hero. Everything hurt.

But riding wasn't an option. The chariots and his donkey were in front, carrying the great prize: the giant's armor and weapons and his huge hoary head.

Saul glanced at his oldest son, his heir. Jonathan was almost as tall as him, but his chest broader and his shoulders wider–wide enough to bear the responsibility. None of his other sons were the warrior Jonathan was. The men who served under his command loved him in a way they didn't love Saul. The tribal leaders wouldn't be able to fault Jonathan on that score when he became king.

The question was what to do about David. He was still young, but he'd done everything Saul asked of him and done it better than veteran soldiers. The men weren't even upset at fighting alongside such a young one.

He came up to Saul's collarbone, but he might grow taller and he'd definitely grow stronger. Armor bearer was a good start.

The front of the army had already reached the village of Azekah and Saul could hear the tambourines and the singing. He clapped David on the shoulder. "Get ready for one of the deepest pleasures of being the victorious army."

Saul smiled in anticipation. Soon, he was close enough to see the women, their heads wrapped in their finest scarves, every necklace they owned clinking on their chests, joy making every one of them beautiful. Their hair gleamed in the sun as they whirled and lifted their tambourines high.

"Look your fill, men, look your fill," Saul called out. "But not so closely that the fathers of Azekah have reason to petition me."

The men around him laughed. David gave the nervous giggle of a boy trying to keep up.

Jonathan skirted behind Saul and held up David's left arm. "Here is the one who defeated the giant with one stone! Here is David, the shield of King Saul!"

Saul grabbed David's right hand and stretched it high.

Azekah's men cheered and the women ran toward Jonathan's voice and then traveled alongside them, singing and dancing.

Saul clapped along until he clued into the words they sang: "Saul has killed his thousands, but David his ten thousands."

His hands froze mid-clap. That couldn't be it. He must have misheard. David hadn't even killed dozens.

But that's what they sang. Saul has killed his thousands, but David his ten thousands. Over and over.

It was like an insect burrowing into his ear. He stared straight ahead, trying not to hear anything.

As king, he could order that there be no more singing. That was within his power.

But nobody feared a king who whined. Besides, he needed the memory of the overwhelming victory and the dancing women to erase that of the forty days of fearful inaction.

Saul shifted his gaze to the left. David was talking under his breath, "That's not right. They can't."

Someone touched Saul's shoulder from behind. Acting on instinct, he spun around and half-unsheathed his sword.

"Hey, it's me."

Saul blinked and saw Abner with his hands in the air. Saul grunted and shoved the sword back in his belt.

Abner pulled up on Saul's right side. "Let's put David up front with the giant's gear."

Could everyone see his reaction to the singing? Could everyone see his weakness?

It was good of Abner to try to lessen the sting of the song for him, but it would be better if the song did not sting. Saul gestured ahead with his chin.

"I'll correct their song, my lord." David had almost slipped through the men in front of them before Abner caught a fistful of David's tunic and hauled him back.

"Don't," Abner ordered the boy.

"But—"

Abner yanked on the tunic again and shook David a little. "You'll dishonor them. This town is under constant threat from the Philistines. They need a hero and today you're it. Now go and stand on the chariot with the armor and smile and flash those pretty brown eyes and make everyone happy by accepting their praise." He shoved David forward none too gently.

David pitched ahead. "Yes, my lord."

Abner rolled his eyes at Saul.

As David disappeared into the ranks of the army, most of the women moved up, parallel with him, but some stayed near Saul. He gritted his teeth and smiled and waved and even threw a few Philistine trinkets their way.

It was the same story in Socoh and then in Gederah, song after song exaggerating David's exploits. Thankfully, after that was a long stretch of no significant population and no more singing.

"It is impossible, of course," Saul said to his son.

"He's new." Jonathan's shrug was good-natured. "A few years ago they sang for me, next time they'll sing for someone else." He leaned close. "But they always sing for you."

Saul snorted. Jonathan had the same tone as when he tried to talk Saul out of his black moods. This was not a black mood. This was a realization: if he was so taken with David that he immediately called him "my shield" and made him an armor bearer, he couldn't blame the people for loving the boy. He wouldn't even blame them if they'd call for David to be king.

That was crazy talk.

He could admit that.

Israel had only had a king for twenty-eight years, but

as a people, they valued stability. One success, no matter how impressive, wasn't enough to get people to call for a new king.

But it might be enough to get certain parties who'd never accepted Saul to try to turn David's head, to cultivate him. David was loyal to his king for now, but what about when he got tired of standing at Saul's side day after day and night after night?

As they neared En-rogel, the last town before home, a song drifted back to him.

How the king rejoices in Your strength, oh Lord!

This tune was one of Saul's favorites. The last time he heard it, a nameless, faceless servant had sung it and he'd reclined on his throne with his eyes closed to better appreciate the music.

It started with the soldiers in front and spread backwards until the entire army, even Jonathan, was praising *Him*. The gruff voices blended with the higher ones. The clear tones of the real singers were audible above the droners.

The king shouts with joy because of Your victory!

It wasn't that Saul wasn't grateful to *Him* for giving them the victory, but why couldn't Saul himself have been more involved in securing it? Even if the only piece of his armor

David had worn had been the helmet, people would have associated the defeat of the giant with his royal symbols. The sight of his blue plume waving as David ran at Goliath would have been a beautiful thing, but no, the boy had to rely on nothing but *Him* and a lousy sling.

The men darted looks Saul's way.

So he wasn't singing along. He was the king.

But then Jonathan guilted him into at least mouthing the words. At En-rogel, he belted them out, mainly in the hopes of blotting out the women's songs.

It didn't work. Now he was stuck singing praises for *His* glory while hearing the women over-praise David.

The last stretch before Gibeah was the worst. The thrill from the victory was gone. His joints complained about the relentless walking. Home felt farther away than when they'd started.

Chatter in the ranks quieted, too. They were all tired. Except for some of the youngest ones. Snippets of conversation made their way to Saul's ears, mostly variations of, "I can't wait to tell my father about David and the giant."

But then he heard, "That must be why Samuel anointed him all those years ago."

His blood turned to ice so quickly it crackled.

Samuel anointed David? Years ago? Did Samuel go around pouring oil over people all around Israel? Was that the source of David's music? Was that why he could defeat the giant? Why would Samuel anoint a child?

The questions were like a wound Saul couldn't leave alone. By the time he got to the fortress, he didn't even want to see his wife. He stomped into his receiving room and turned his face to the wall. Someone put food down next to him, so he put some in his mouth. The raisin cakes tasted moldy and the wine like it had already turned to vinegar. He kicked the dishes over.

His wife came in and stroked his shoulders and his hair. He shook her off. When she didn't take the hint, he pushed her away.

People milled about, telling him what he needed. Jonathan said he needed rest. His wife said he needed to soak in some warm water. Abner said he needed wine. Servants piled bowl after bowl of treats in front of him.

If one more person presumed to know the mind of the king, he was going to grab his spear. It took all his discipline to use his too-calm voice. "I need to be alone."

They gasped, but followed his order. Finally he was alone. Not at peace, but alone.

It was morning, but still dark when he bellowed for a servant.

One of his armor bearers stepped into the room from his overnight post by the doorway, but it was too dark to see which one. "Is that you, David?"

"No, my lord."

"Bring him to me."

"He's asleep. Shall I wake him?"

Saul let the silence grow until the man knew what a mistake he'd made. "No delays, do you hear me?"

"Yes, my lord. No delay."

The sky was still mostly dark when David finally arrived.

"You're across the courtyard. What took so long?"

David cleared his throat. "My morning, um, functions, my lord."

"Piss on your own time," Saul said. "Now that you're a great hero and the new hope of all Israel, are you too important to play the lyre for your king?"

David bowed at the waist. "I serve at the pleasure of Adonai's Anointed One. Always."

The pleasure Saul usually got from David's name for him turned to ashes in his ears. "Just play."

Instead of the smooth and beautiful tunes David usually drew from his lyre, it sounded like disjointed plinking, and his voice was rough and scratchy.

So what if David had fought and killed Philistines for three days, marched all day yesterday, singing half the time, and then was woken at dawn from a dead sleep. Saul needed him to be at the top of his game, so he'd better figure out how to get there.

"Is there a problem?" Saul asked.

"Of, of course not, my lord."

"Don't be ridiculous. You're on the verge of falling down."

"Perhaps some water."

"Bring his exaltedness a bowl of goat's milk," Saul called.

"I'm fine with wa–"

Saul picked up his spear and pounded it on the floor to shut the boy up. He stared at the ceiling until a servant brought the milk and David drank it. The same servant or a different one, it didn't matter, lit several lamps.

The pious little twit started with the Shema. Of course David would start the day doing right by *Him*.

From there, it got worse. It used to be that the nameless, faceless servant's songs lifted Saul up and filled him with a sense of oneness, of confidence, of possibility. Now that he knew that the songs were David's, his own inadequacies became sharper. Even though his eyes were closed, he could still see David striding to meet the giant dressed in a plain tunic and armed with a sling and a staff while he stood in the crowd, ineffectual, unnecessary.

But he needed the music. He needed it to work.

As David warmed up, the sounds became as beautiful as they used to be, and the rougher voice made the words seem even more heartfelt. David sang song after song about *Him* rescuing *His* people until Saul was on the verge of tears.

Saul tapped the end of his spear on the floor several times. "*He* saves, but *His* burden is so heavy."

David kept playing, but he stopped singing.

"Let me tell you what it feels like to disappoint *Him*, because you're young, you're riding high, and you think *He* will be with you always." Saul tugged at the strings in his tassel. "If you thought this battle was a bloodbath, you should've seen what we did to the Amalekites ten years ago. Samuel told me *He* wanted them all slaughtered and we did our job. We destroyed them."

He closed his eyes and saw the scene again. "Some streets literally ran with blood. We showed no mercy."

Saul crushed the tassel in his fist. "How did Samuel think I was going to pay the men for the time it took to gather two hundred thousand troops and march to Amalek, the seven days for the Kenites to move out of the way, and then the days it took to march almost all the way to Egypt, killing our way through all those Amalekite villages and walled cities? How was I to compensate them except through plunder? So the men kept some goods. We were going to sacrifice a portion of them."

The music was sad and plaintive, which spurred on Saul's tirade.

"Was that good enough for *Him*?" He threw the tassel down. "No. Samuel went on and on about obedience, about how following *His* 'requests' were better than the best sacrifices. Like that would have gone over well with the tired and hungry men. Or with their wives."

The music stopped. Saul opened his eyes.

David was still there. Saul could see the pity, the easy judgment, the arrogance of youth staring back at him. He knew the boy was thinking that he'd never go against *His* requests. That David honored his king enough not to condemn him to his face made it worse.

Talking about the Amalekite disaster jogged his memory. Samuel told him something back then. Something big. What was it?

Now he had it.

After Saul debased himself by begging Samuel not to embarrass him, Samuel raked him over the coals about the Amalekites said that the kingdom of Israel was torn from him, that the Lord had already given it to someone else, someone better.

At the time, there was no one better. But now...

Here was this boy who did amazing things yet had the humility of a servant. Who gave all the glory to *Him*.

Someone else, someone better.

Someone who praised with the passion of an angel. Someone who fought like a sandstorm. Someone whom Samuel had anointed.

Before he had time to register it as a plan, Saul changed to a throwing grip on his spear and launched it.

13. The first spear

The spear skidded to the ground two handspans from David, who stared at it, his eyes wide, before bolting from the room, his feet scrambling for purchase.

Saul swallowed and tasted blood. He must have bitten his tongue.

Did he try to kill David?

Surely not. His aim with the spear was unerring. If he'd wanted to kill David, the boy would be dead. It was battle weariness. Frustration with a victory that wasn't a true victory for him. That had to be it.

That he derived a small bit of pleasure from imagining David pinned to the wall by his spear was better ignored.

Jonathan tore through the doorway. "What's going on? Are you in danger?"

Saul threw his hands in the air and feigned distress. "There's been a terrible misunderstanding. I was telling David an old story and I got so frustrated with the past that I threw my spear. It got close to David, but I wasn't trying to harm him. You know how the young jump to conclusions. You know how good I am with the spear. Find him, talk to him, bring him back to me."

Jonathan didn't even blink before he said, "Yes, Father," and ran after David.

And then all Saul could do was wait to see whether his son was as good a diplomat as he was a warrior.

*****

David staggered into the courtyard and tore through the servants' room and the kitchen, as far as he could get from Saul while remaining in the compound. He leaned back against the outside wall. His chest heaved. Pinpricks of light swam in his vision.

Had the king tried to kill him?

What other explanation could there be?

Why? What had he ever done to King Saul?

These last four days were the best of his life. His anointing finally made sense. Could it all be ripped away from him so soon?

Other servants rushed in and out of the storeroom, preparing breakfast. He turned toward the wall.

What would happen if he went to the king, fell to his knees and bowed low, as low as he did when he first came to Gibeah, and asked what he'd done to offend the Lord's Anointed, to please tell him so he could fix it?

A big show had always made his father angrier, but maybe Saul would respond better.

David was still imagining and reimagining this scene when Jonathan found him and pulled him into a hug. "Little brother, it'll be okay." He kept one arm around

David's shoulders and guided him around the outside of the building, to the alley. "My father says he was upset because of the story he was telling. He didn't mean for the spear to come anywhere near you."

That was possible. Whatever his reasons were, Saul had disobeyed the Lord and argued with the prophet. David couldn't imagine anything more upsetting than that.

"Haven't you ever lashed out when you're frustrated?"

David nodded. Any interaction with Eliab always made him want to go into the hills and whip rocks at stuff. The king could have had the same kind of reaction, except with a spear instead of a sling. "He is known for his aim."

"You see. You know that it wasn't anything personal. If he'd aimed it at you and tried to, you know, he would've succeeded."

David gave a halfhearted shrug.

Jonathan unwound his cloak. It wasn't one of the ceremonial garments he wore to important dinners, but it did have blue-dyed side hems and embroidered olive branches on the top and bottom edges. "Take it. As a symbol of our friendship and of the esteem my family holds for you."

David looked down. "It's an honor too great for me."

"I'm going to drop it now." Jonathan held it at arm's length. "It'll either go to you or to the dust."

David caught it long before it hit the ground.

It was the most beautiful garment he had ever touched.

The linen was finer than anything the wealthiest family in Bethlehem owned. He folded it without letting it touch his battle-stained tunic.

"It's not going to bite you." Jonathan snatched it, shook it out and draped it over David's shoulders. "Let's go see my father so we can get back to normal."

"But the edges will get dirty."

"That's what edges are for."

Still, David bunched it in his fists so it wouldn't drag. They walked across the fortress in silence.

Was Jonathan telling the truth? Or was he leading David to his death and this beautiful garment was to be his shroud?

Whatever his fate, he would meet it with honor.

David's heart thudded. Jonathan had made it sound like David could expect an apology. But the king never admitted fault, even when he was in the wrong. Not even when he'd gone against Samuel and the Lord.

He should stick with the original plan and grovel even though he was blameless. His only other option was to return to Bethlehem. After something as huge as killing that giant, Jesse might make him sleep in the sheepfold, just to make sure he knew his place. Acting guilty and throwing himself on the mercy of the king had to be better than that.

When they reached the receiving room, the king rose and opened his arms wide. David sunk to his knees and dipped until his forehead tapped the floor. "If I've done anything to anger the Lord's Anointed, tell me so I can cut off the offending part."

"Your humility is commendable, as usual," Saul said. "Get up."

That was not a gentle request. David stood, but kept his gaze on the king's throwing hand.

"Get ready to take your shift as my armor bearer. We need to get to Gilgal well before nightfall. Every victory doesn't inspire a peace offering of thanksgiving, but this is a special case." Saul's lips were curved up, but it wasn't a reassuring smile.

"Yes, my king." What else could David say?

"Doesn't David look fine in my cloak?" Jonathan asked.

Saul raised his eyebrows. "First your sword, your belt, and your tunic on the battlefield, and now this."

"It's a symbol of–"

"I know what it is," Saul said.

David held his breath as Saul and Jonathan had some kind of intense yet silent communication.

"It will not do, of course, for you to wear the cloak in the course of your duties, but Jonathan is free to give you what he wishes." Saul dismissed them with a flick of his hand and David blew out a sigh.

"What did I tell you," Jonathan said once they were outside. "Everything's fine."

David was pretty sure neither of them believed that.

By the time David returned to the kitchen courtyard, all that was left of the morning meal was half a round of stale bread and a pool of whey in the bottom of a bowl. Not nearly enough, but he wolfed down the bread and drank down the dregs of the yoghurt and rushed back to his new quarters on the second floor.

Nobody was there. Good.

He folded the linen flat and slipped it under his bedroll. It wasn't that he was ashamed, but he didn't want to have to explain how he got such a fancy piece of clothing.

He grabbed his belt, his water skin, and his smallest lyre and strapped them on top of his tunic.

The king had told him to hurry, but if they were heading for Gilgal, there was one more thing he needed to take. One thing he needed to sacrifice to the Lord. David wrapped its long belt around each shoulder where the sled leads had gone. His rope burn had faded, but not enough, and it hurt. He undid it and then tried it around his chest, but his skin was bad there, too, and now the tip of the giant sword scraped the ground and dragged as bad as the sled had. He redid the wrapping again, threw his regular cloak on top of everything, and headed for the tower stairs.

The sword smacked the back of his calves with every step. It was sheathed, so he didn't get cut up, but he couldn't handle that the whole walk to Gilgal. When he shortened his stride, it was better, but he'd look like a kid scampering after the adult goats.

He could leave the cloak off, but then it'd be the walk to Gibeah all over again, everyone making a big deal about him. A *good Israelite takes no glory for himself.* His father was right about that. Better to hide the sword than spend the next few hours exhausting himself trying to deflect the people's praise to Adonai, where it belonged.

The king was already yelling for him. David stumbled down the stairs and through the back hall. "Here I am, my lord."

"About time." Saul thrust his shield at David. "Clean and polish this until it'll blind people."

The oil pot and cloths were behind the throne, so David had to walk past the king to get there.

"What's wrong with your cloak?"

The king was in the kind of mood when it was better to say nothing than the wrong thing.

"Don't just stand there. Get to work. We leave as soon as Abner gets here."

There was still blood and mud crusted on the shield, so David added some grit from the floor to the oil and scoured the most stubborn bits. Abner came before he was done, so David had to buff it with his cloak hem as they marched. He didn't finish until they reached the main road.

Even after he showed Saul the shield with its copper

plating gleaming, the king still glowered. "Why are you walking that way?"

"I'm carrying something on my back." It was beyond awkward, holding the king's shield with his right hand and reaching back with his left to keep the sword from bumping his legs.

Saul opened David's cloak wide enough to see the sword. His neck became as mottled as a gecko's back. "Leave it here."

David gulped. "The Lord put it on my heart to make Him an offering."

Saul sucked in air through his teeth. "You can hardly move." He raised his hand. David flinched, but all Saul did was yell for another armor bearer.

David handed over the shield and dropped back. Someone snickered and shoved his shoulder from behind. The sword got tangled in his tunic and he had to hop to keep himself from falling. This morning had been one humiliation after another.

Eliab poked at the package on David's back. "What are you trying to hide?"

David pulled his cloak tighter, which mashed the sword against him, restricting his movement even more.

"You're not too high and mighty for me to put you in a headlock, you know," Eliab said.

Instinctively, David ducked his head and sidestepped away.

Eliab laughed. "Glad you still know your place." He kicked at the lump behind David's legs.

"Stop it! That's the giant's sword."

"Let me see it."

"You had three days to see it if you wanted to."

"Aw. Poor little David is sad his brother didn't come and bow before him like everyone else."

"People are staring."

Eliab snorted. "You're going to have to be tougher than that if you want to stay in the army."

David wouldn't look at his brother. "It's in its sheath. You'll see it when we get there."

Somehow, Eliab was satisfied with that. Or, at least, he stopped hassling David.

The road was packed. Families were loaded down with animals and grain for the sacrifice and wine and food for the feast. A boy around Asahel's age loped alongside the army, begging them to show him their weapons and their spoils.

Eliab piped up, "Did you hear how we won?"

"A boy not much older than me cut the head off the Philistine giant." The boy said it with such gusto.

"Would you like to meet him?" Eliab asked.

"Would I ever."

What was going on? Eliab never drew attention to David unless he could benefit. What was his angle?

"Right here." Eliab pointed at David.

The boy went into spasms of excitement.

David tried to maintain the hard look of a serious soldier, but the boy's joy was infectious. He smiled.

"You're so amazing."

"The Lord gave me victory," David said. "He's always there for those who call on Him."

"I can't believe it's you, that you're right here. My father has to meet you. Please come back and say hello to my father. He'll never believe me otherwise."

"I'd love to," David lied, "but my responsibilities keep me here."

"Please, please, please. I'm sure he'll give you some of our silver or something."

The boy's pleading made David grit his teeth. "I'm an armor bearer now and I need to stay close to the king. Maybe I'll see you at the sacrifices." He fixed his gaze on the road ahead.

"Okay." The boy stopped running and David marched past him.

As soon as David thought the boy was out of earshot, he rounded on his brother. "Don't do that ag–"

"Have some bread or something," Eliab said. "You're cranky."

David couldn't help rolling his eyes.

"You do have food, don't you?"

"No."

"Do you think the army brought any food for us?" Eliab

didn't wait for an answer. "Well, they didn't. They expect us to do half a day's march in the blazing sun with no mid-day meal. You can't just be the youngest son here. Mother isn't here to make sure there's enough for you."

"With all these people, someone will show hospitality."

"How right you are." Eliab smiled and melted out of sight.

A fist-sized lump of dread lodged itself in David's chest. His brother's smiles rarely meant good news for him.

They still headed north on a wide track. The terrain reminded him of home: brown and hilly, crisscrossed by dry wadi beds and dotted by rock outcrops, with only an occasional scrubby tree. Wearing a cloak on a day march during the heat season with no shade was not a wise decision. By the time the sun was high, David's tunic was three shades darker from sweat.

And then the road angled down. When the road went up, the walking was easier, because his legs moved away from the sword, but now that they were headed down, it was constantly in the way. He took a heavy step over a hole. On landing, the sword jabbed the tendon behind his foot. Pain hobbled him and he crumpled.

This was stupid.

There was no point in half killing himself in order to remain anonymous. He shucked off the cloak and shifted the bindings until the sword hung from his right shoulder, down his side. He tied his cloak around his waist, creating a buffer between his leg and the sword. Not ideal, but it was better.

As David turned from the northern to the eastern road, he heard someone yelling his name. He turned far enough around that he was walking backwards before he saw Eliab's head bobbing above the crowd. David spun around to face front.

"I've got someone I want you to meet," Eliab said.

"Who?"

"You'll see."

"No."

"I'll tell Abner that I need to talk to you about family business and you'll have to come with me. Oldest brother always wins."

The story of his life. David let his brother lead him against the river of people until they reached a wealthy-looking family.

Eliab boomed, "Here he is," and put his hand on David's shoulder, digging in with his fingers. "The one who killed the giant and rallied Israel to victory."

"It's an honor and a blessing to meet you," the man said.

David inclined his head. "The Lord handed the giant to me. The victory is His. Where are you from?"

The man ignored him; he only had eyes for the sword. "Is that it? May I see it?"

David studied the limbs of a tree above the man's head. It wouldn't be hard to raise the flap and lift the sword a bit, but the idea opened up a pit in his middle. Or maybe that was hunger. "I vowed that I wouldn't unwrap it until I presented it to the Lord at Gilgal."

"Come on." Eliab's voice was brittle although he was smiling. "One peek won't hurt."

"You'd have me break a sacred vow?" David gave a short bow to the man. "I'm sorry. I hope you enjoy the rest of your journey."

Before David rejoined the crowd, he caught part of their conversation. "You promised." "You met him and saw it." "I want my payment back."

David's tongue thickened in his mouth. He wanted to stalk back there and tell off Eliab for using Adonai's glory for his own gain. Instead, he prayed, "Forgive me for lying to that man. I vow it before You now."

How could Eliab sell him out like that? Did the people around him see what had happened? Were they judging him? Should he say something? If he railed against his brother in public, it would bring shame on the entire family.

"You've got to do better next time." Eliab was back. "Show a little personality."

"There won't be a next time." David shifted the sword to the side away from his brother. "You're always on me for showing off and now you *want* me to?"

"Now it works for me. I'm hungry." Eliab snorted. "If you want to wait until after the ceremony to eat, be my guest.

I'm capitalizing on a situation. To show there are no hard feelings, here's your share."

Nestled in his hand were four figs and a strip of bread. The figs' skin was a deep, dull, wrinkly purple. They'd be sweet and ripe and juicy.

Now that food was in front of him, he was ravenous. He didn't want to encourage Eliab or benefit from his scheme, but he couldn't last until evening without taking in anything.

"It's mine in 5, 4, 3, 2–"

David snatched it.

"I knew you'd see reason."

The ill-gained food should have tasted like dust, but it was delicious. David crammed the bread in his mouth, but took his time with the figs, savoring each one.

His brother did it twice more. Each time, David grew more withdrawn. The third time, when Eliab offered him the food, David knocked it out of his hand without speaking and stalked away, not caring how unwieldy the sword was or how many people he bumped into.

By the time he'd calmed down enough to notice his surroundings, the sun was far behind him in the west. The trees were taller, and there was more underbrush. The road brought them higher and higher. Finally, they reached the top of a ridge. David gasped.

14. Sacrifices

In front of David was the widest and flattest valley he'd ever seen. In the middle was a winding thick green band. Hidden in all that vegetation must be the River Jordan. He stepped to the side of the road to take it all in.

Right there was where his ancestors had crossed over on dry ground into the Promised Land after forty years of wandering. Down there was Jericho, where the Lord made the walls fall down at the blast of the shofar.

Between the river and Jericho was Gilgal. Joshua and the people camped there, built an altar there, celebrated the first Passover feast right there. Samuel judged the people there. The people gathered and crowned Saul king with feasts and sacrifices.

He frowned down at the city. If he'd pieced together the king's story right, Samuel had threatened to leave Saul high and dry in front of a crowd like the one he was in right now. No wonder he'd lashed out this morning with his spear. It hadn't been personal. David had been in the wrong place at the wrong time. His nagging doubts melted away and David jumped down the ridge like a goat.

This was going to be even better than the night after he'd killed Goliath. He was going to see priests in their ceremonial clothes do a ritual sacrifice. He was going to worship Adonai with thousands of people. He might even see Samuel and ask him whether the anointing was to prepare him for the giant.

David cocked his head and listened.

Last time he'd wondered about that, he heard The Voice.

This time, he heard plenty of voices, as well as the wind and the footfall of soldiers and donkeys, the creaking of carts and rumbling of wheels. But not The Voice.

When Gilgal's walls were within his sights, travel came to a standstill. He skirted the road on the left and stood where he could watch people go through the gates.

The doors were thrown wide open, and a priest stood on a raised platform on one side. "People with lambs, go to the right pillar. Goats use the left pillar. Oxen, go all the way around on the right side. Do not enter the meeting with the whole animal. Cup of blood and fat only. Bags of grain here with me," he bent down to bless someone leaving grain, "but take your portion for the altar." He repeated this as people filed through the gates.

A voice from the crowd called out, "There he is! The giant killer!"

Heads craned around and then hands pulled him into the sea of people. He was hugged and bounced and kissed on the cheek by more people than he could count. The dreaded song started up: "Saul has killed his thousands, but David his ten thousands."

Please let the king not be able to hear it.

David lost his bearings as he was passed from person to person, group to group. They pinched and elbowed him. His hair was repeatedly snagged. He had to hug the sword to his front to prevent it from being pulled away. This was way more chaotic than battle.

When a commanding voice shouted, "Move it! Make way for the army commander," David groaned in relief.

He pushed his way toward Abner's voice.

"There you are." Abner hooked David's elbow and David followed in his wake until they were free from the crowd.

"I was getting eaten alive," David said at the same time as Abner said, "Don't revel in your glory too much."

"What?" David shook his head to clear his brain. "I wasn't doing that."

Abner gave him an irritated glance. "You should. It'd make you seem more human."

That made no sense. What was he, if not human?

As soon as they approached the hip-height wall around the meeting area, what David saw made him forget his confusion.

"Stop squirming."

"Can't I watch a few sacrifices?"

"You'll see plenty when we're in there." Abner tightened his grip.

David planted his feet and leaned back.

Abner glared at him, but then his expression softened. "Alright. I remember my first time." He crossed his arms and stood back.

David gaped at the scene, but managed a distracted, "Thanks."

They stood near the right pillar, where people brought their lambs. The father of the family presented the animal to the priest, who inspected it. If he approved of it, the father moved to the right and slit the lamb's throat, letting the blood drain into a channel at the base of the wall, except for one small bowlful, which was placed to the side. When that was done, they moved farther to the right because another family was already waiting to slit their lamb's throat.

The rest of the family joined the father in butchering the lamb. In what seemed like several blinks of David's eyes, the task was done. The father gave the right thigh and breast to a different priest, who handed it off to a runner. The flesh to be cooked for the feast went to another runner, who brought it to cooking vats with steam curling to the sky. The fat and internal organs went on a platter that the family carried into the meeting with their bowl of blood.

David let Abner lead him like one of the lambs while he took everything in. The line of worshippers carrying their bowls and platters, waiting their turn in front of the altar.

The hewn stone altar, not the one Joshua made of river stone, but large enough to hold a whole heifer. The three priests at the altar, one on the right taking the bowls of blood and tossing the contents on the side corners, one on the left accepting the platters of fat and organs and dumping them on the fire, and one at the back speaking a blessing to each family.

Between the crowd and the thick smoke billowing and flames flaring high, David had a hard time making out the priests. He caught a glimpse of the blue of their cloaks, but that was about it.

Abner stopped moving and let go of him. They were right behind the king and his family, next to the tribal leaders and military commanders. Abner must be getting some instructions from the king and then they'd go to where David should be.

David waited, but Abner didn't speak to the king and they didn't move on.

This wasn't the place for him. He should be wherever the other soldiers were, unless he was pulling his armor bearer duty, which nobody was directing him to do.

He skittered backwards, but Abner caught his forearm.

"But–"

"You plan to unsheath the sword before you offer it?"

David nodded.

"It would be a danger to the people if you had to walk all the way from the back."

That made sense, but it felt wrong. If his father were here, he'd give David such a talking to for thinking he was on a par with the king now. Even though he didn't.

Abner didn't drop his hand until the priest behind the altar stepped out of the smoke.

It wasn't Samuel.

High Priest Ahimelech was impressive, but he wasn't Samuel. David hadn't realized how much he'd been looking forward to seeing the prophet, to asking him about that anointing, until it was clear that wouldn't happen.

It was such a visual feast that David couldn't wallow in disappointment for long. The reality was so much more colorful than what he'd imagined from his grandfather Obed's descriptions. The High Priest wore deep blue linen with embroidered red, blue, and purple pomegranates alternating with gold bells around the hem of the cloak. A blue turban with a gold plate on the front rose above his forehead. It was magnificent, but it all paled next to the ephod. Everything about the ephod was gold: the shoulder straps, the cords, the breastplate, everything except the twelve precious stones for the twelve tribes. The fire on the altar reflected off the ephod and light flashed over the crowd.

As Ahimelech praised Adonai for delivering His people yet again, the setting sun made the ephod gleam orange and the gems flash. David couldn't stop staring. A breeze blew the sickly sweet smoke over David's section. His head wobbled and he shook it to try and keep his focus, but soon he canted to the side and barely stopped himself from falling over.

"Bend your knees." Abner poked the backs of David's knees with the toe of his sandal. "If you lock your knees, you'll go down and dishonor your king and your father."

David dutifully bent his knees, but he also twisted around and scanned the crowd behind him. "My father's here?" It seemed like a year had passed since he'd seen his family, although it had been less than a week.

Abner turned David until he faced front again.

"He hasn't come here for a sacrifice since he was in the army."

Abner gave him one of those looks that adults gave children when they were saying too many things at once.

"Because of me?"

"Every man here wishes you were his son."

If that's what Abner thought, he didn't know Jesse at all.

Ahimelech recited in a voice loud enough to break through David's thoughts, "Listen, O Israel! Adonai is our God, Adonai alone." He repeated it and the crowd settled.

David shivered as he and everyone else joined in, "And you must love Adonai with all your heart, all your soul, and all your strength. "

Right then, they were truly one with Adonai and with each other. The truth of it hummed through David's body.

When the echo of the last word faded, the king went

forward, and then Jonathan, each presenting a pure white lamb and going behind the altar to kill and butcher it. They presented the blood and fat and the fire flared again. The tribal leaders did the same.

And then Abner pushed him forward.

Panic flared in David's chest as hot as the fire on the altar. He dug his heels in.

"No," David whispered. "I'm only—"

"Do it or I'll carry you up there," Abner said. "The Lord deserves His firstfruits and the people deserve to see it."

David stepped into the aisle. He fumbled with the sheath flap and then drew out the sword until he couldn't raise his arm any higher. The sword was double-edged, so he couldn't take it out the rest of the way hand over hand. His free hand scrabbled over the ties. He had to get this sheath off him, but the belt was wrapped around him so many times.

The crowd was silent. He could feel the pressure of all those pairs of eyes on him, greedy for a look at the sword.

After an age, the straps unwound.

The iron was hot where he rested it on the flats of his palms and walked forward. His biceps were shaking by the time he reached the priest, but he straightened his arms as best he could, and handed over the sword of Goliath.

The priest didn't smile. He took it as soberly as David

offered it. A cheer went up as Ahimelech grasped the hilt in both hands and raised the sword above his head.

David tipped his head back to look at it one more time.

There was no rush of euphoria or astonishment at what he'd done with that sword. He didn't lift his fist or jeer at the Philistines as the crowd did.

It was right. That was all.

It was right that Adonai triumphed over those who mocked Him. David played a part, but any one of these men could have done it if they'd trusted Him. And it was right that the sword was in the possession of Adonai, since He was the one who gave David the power to use it.

"To the faithful, You show Yourself faithful," David said, although nobody could hear him. "Praise Your holy name forever."

It is you.

The hair on his arms stood on end. That was The Voice.

Like last time, "It is you," was all it said.

What did it mean?

Abner pulled David back to the king's section as dozens of hands slapped his back.

With that, the official portion of the evening was over. Those who needed to present their blood and fat lined up, but everyone else streamed out, calling out the kind of meat they'd brought, yelling for lost family members.

Outside the low wall, some men took out instruments and played them, singing rollicking songs that got knots of people raising their hands and dancing.

Now that lids were coming off pots, and breads and cheeses were being taken out of their wrappers, David could smell and see what he was missing. His eyes glazed and he weaved on his feet again. He bent his knees, which made him more stable, but didn't do anything about the overwhelming appeal of that food.

David had to blink and work hard to focus on what the men around the king were saying to him.

"...elder of Manasseh," said a man with long white hair. "It is an honor to meet a young man of such obvious faith." He squeezed David's face and kissed his cheeks.

As the other tribal leaders did the same thing, and even while David said and did all the appropriate things in return, he could hear people calling from all over, "Jesse ben Obed of Bethlehem! Jesse ben Obed of Bethlehem!" They were looking for his father to bring him here to meet the king.

The tribal leaders kept talking to him, but David's gaze kept sliding to the pillars, which should have been considered rude, but they looked indulgent, not upset.

And then his father paused at the entrance.

David fought two childish urges: to cry, for what, he didn't know, and to apologize for losing the skins he'd made the sled out of.

King Saul called, "This must be Jesse, father of David. We thank the Lord for fathers who raise their sons right."

Jesse dipped his head and then spread his arms to indicate all of David's brothers. "My family has always fought proudly for Israel."

Saul smiled. "You could populate half a unit by yourself. May your sons be as fruitful in sons as you were."

"I am grateful to do my very small part," Jesse said.

"Very small!" Saul elbowed Abner. "'Very small,' he said." Saul looked David up and down. "I admit, he's not the tallest of my men, but he makes up for it in bravery."

Everyone laughed politely, but when Saul kept being amused at his own joke, they had to keep going, too.

Saul stopped abruptly and clapped his hands. "But now it is time to eat. I expect you and your family to join us."

"My lord and king," Jesse said, "your offer is kind and gracious, but we are–"

"You would deny the king such a simple request?" Saul stood over a head taller than Jesse, and when he raised his eyebrows and stared down, he seemed even taller than that. "The table is ready."

They sat where they were told to, on the bottom end of the mats, away from the king and his family, with the tribal leaders and military officers between them.

Jesse and David's brothers fidgeted, their eyes darting around, trying to look like they weren't whispering to each other. If David didn't know better, he'd think they were worried.

David pressed his lips together to keep from gloating. They *were* nervous. They didn't know what to do. And he did. Even though he'd only observed dinners with the king, the youngest brother was the expert and they'd have to listen to him.

He leaned forward and whispered, "Wait for the servants to bring out all the food. Don't eat until they start." He nodded toward the dignitaries without looking at them. "Copy whatever they do."

During dinner there were numerous speeches: to the king, to each of the military commanders and tribal leaders, to David, to Jesse, to the army in general. With every speech, they lifted their cups and drank. By the middle of the meal, the mood at the table was a good deal looser. Nethanel and Raddai stopped looking at David out of the corners of their eyes, as if trying to figure out what kind of strange thing he'd become, and treated him normally. His father even laughed when David apologized for losing the skins.

By the end of the meal, there was more singing, and people were up and moving, but it wasn't dancing so much as staggering and lurching. Torches were lit so the celebration could continue.

There was a flurry of movement from the king's end of the mats. Runners were called in and then sent out.

Saul stood, so the rest of them did, too.

"I have some important news," Saul said. "Follow me." He climbed on top of the short wall next to the right-hand pillar. Jonathan went up next to him.

David, his family, and the dignitaries waited at their feet while runners spread the word and everyone else filed in.

"People of Israel," Saul shouted. "We have celebrated our victory against the Philistines."

Half the crowd cheered and the other half spat.

"As your king, I need to ensure that we defeat them every time." Saul paused while the people shouted their agreement. "And the Ammonites, the Amalekites, the Geshurites, and the Moabites. *All* the enemies of the Lord's people."

They pumped their fists in the air and jumped up and down.

"Our enemies are growing and getting stronger, so we need to, as well." Saul looked slowly over the crowd. "We need a permanent army. Men who train year-round, all tribes together. The Lord is one, and we need to be one."

David drove one fist into the other palm. Finally. This was what Israel needed to do to once and for all conquer their enemies. He grinned so hard his face hurt, because, as an armor bearer, he'd get to be part of it all. He'd get to openly train with the army. Thanks to Jonathan, he had the beginnings of his own equipment. If he could figure out how to cut down the giant's armor to fit him, he wouldn't have to use poor man's armor. He wouldn't have to burden his family.

"Here are your military leaders," Saul said. "My son Jonathan."

The people cheered.

"Commander Abner."

Abner climbed up next to Jonathan.

The people cheered.

Five more men climbed up on the wall to be introduced, and each time, the people cheered.

David was still applauding the leader from Gad when the king called his name. His brothers pushed him from behind and hands grasped his and hauled him up. Before he knew what was happening, he was standing on the wall between Jonathan and Abner. The sound of blood rushing through his ears almost drowned out the sound of the crowd. What was the king doing?

"You all know of David, our giant slayer!" Saul yelled.

The people danced and shouted while Jonathan held up David's left arm and Abner his right.

"What say you to this?" Saul continued. "David shall have his own command and his own men."

"But, but–" David was drowned out by the approval of the people. This was wrong. It was all wrong.

15. Joining the giant slayer's unit

David tried desperately to catch Abner's eye. He was only just barely in the army. How could he command a unit?

Saul called out, "Who wants the honor of serving under the giant killer?"

Many men surged forward, but his brothers slunk to the side.

"It's too much, my lord." David didn't care that he sounded like a terrified boy.

Saul must not have heard, because he addressed the crowd again. "There are so many of you. How shall we determine this? Cast lots? Wrestling? That's it. Wrestling. David deserves to lead the strongest and the toughest. Come to the front!"

"But I'm not qualified for this," David said to the air.

"Nonsense," Abner said. "You've been hanging around during training and you proved yourself on the battlefield this week."

"It may sound exciting to them now, but in the light of day, they'll have to take orders from a sixteen-year-old."

"Lighten up." Jonathan slapped David's back. "Don't underestimate the bragging rights those men will have."

"Your king asks this of you." Abner spoke in a threatening rumble. "Are you or are you not his servant?"

As burly soldiers shoved their way to the wall, David wanted to scream that it was all a joke or a bad dream, anything to get it to stop, but how could he contradict the king in front of a crowd that had been drinking wine for hours?

Jonathan leaned close to David. "Don't worry about it. You're a natural leader."

Two soldiers whose chests were as massive as a bull's were bouncing off each other, boasting nonstop. Those on the outskirts were egging them on.

"I don't want anyone to get hurt." David sent Jonathan a pleading glance. The soldiers were maybe a half step removed from an unruly mob. Someone had to get through to the king.

Jonathan sighed. "Father."

"A lively bunch, don't you think?" Saul sounded pleased.

"The men are exhausted, over-full, and probably drunk."

The smile stayed on Saul's face, but his voice was sharp. "Are you telling me my order is wrong?"

Jonathan stared resolutely ahead. "I'm just concerned for the men."

"And I am not?"

Jonathan cleared his throat.

"I see." Saul's voice was tight and shaky.

David panted as if he'd run full out through the city. He went to step down, but Saul's hand shot behind Jonathan and held David's upper arm in an unshakable grip.

"The competition is about to begin." Saul spoke softly, but the menace in his tone made David shiver.

Jonathan murmured to David, "Remember. You have something stronger than the rest of us."

David frowned up at Jonathan. What was he talking about?

Jonathan mouthed, "The Lord."

Fear was making David's throat close, but he swallowed hard, licked his lips, and said, "I've played for the Lord way longer than I've been a soldier. Can't I lead worshippers instead?"

The longer Saul was still, the harder David's heart beat and the more restless the men got. There was going to be no way out of it. He was going to have to stand there and watch men beat themselves to a bloody pulp for him.

Without warning, Saul snapped, "Fine. Take out your lyre." He raised his voice and addressed the crowd. "I see before me the strongest and the toughest soldiers of any generation."

Everyone roared in approval.

"You want to fight for the honor to serve under David."

David's stomach clenched as they bellowed again.

Saul stretched his arms forward. "You already did."

A few people whooped, but more people grumbled and looked up with confused frowns.

"What is your first order?" Saul yelled at David.

David sent up a silent prayer for Adonai to save him, to not let him fall on his face, and then he raised the lyre above his head and strummed the strings. "Rejoice."

He should have asked Adonai to not let his voice crack. It was going to have to stop doing that if he was going to be any kind of military leader. He cleared his throat and tilted his head back. "Songs of joy and victory are sung in the camp of the godly. Rejoice, I say!"

He'd never sung for a drunken throng who'd been denied their blood-lust, but he played the liveliest tune he could think of and sang, "Sing praises to God and to His name." He took it up a notch. "Sing praises to Him who rides the clouds. His name is Adonai. Rejoice!"

People stared at him as if he had two heads, but he kept singing. He jumped off the wall and snaked his way through the crowd, praying that even one person would follow his lead. Out of the corner of his eye he saw Abinadab and Shammah link arms and squeeze in behind him. Eventually, more men linked arms or clapped their hands in the air and fell in line.

David spun around, his lyre high above his head, and spotted the king, as still and rigid as the wall he stood on, his eyebrows a dark line across his forehead. There was no time to worry about the king's disapproval, though;

David still had to win the approval of the men who were now pushing him forward.

He had no idea where to go once they were through the pillars and in the village proper, so he wound them through the streets. His voice was rough and the men were mumbling more than singing, but then a woman's high, clear tone joined in the melody. To his right, a woman his mother's age stood behind a low gate, smiling. An oil lamp rested on the wall next to her.

"If the music weren't so beautiful, I'd scold you for keeping up my grandchildren," she said.

"I'm sorry." Although he wasn't. "Do you know a place my soldiers and I can rest for the night?"

"Anyone who sings so well for the Lord is welcome anytime." She opened the gate and ushered them through. "The house can't hold everyone, but the ground under the olive tree is soft. You may come inside with me."

"I stay with my men," he replied in a monotone.

She insisted, but he held firm. He knew little about being a military leader, but with seven older brothers, he knew plenty about groups of men. There would be no accepting special treatment until he'd proved himself worthy, and maybe not even then.

As soon as she left them, he drew his cloak over his head and pretended to be instantly asleep, but his thoughts whirled half the night with imagined scenes of his men laughing at their late-night folly and leaving him in disgrace in the morning. What could he do to get them to stay?

As soon as the sky was half-bright, he lifted his covering just high enough to see out.

The men were stirring. A few of them were sitting up and rubbing their temples.

He pushed himself upright. "Good morning," was the first brilliant thing out of his mouth.

They mumbled their return greetings.

David got his first good look at them.

There were forty-six men, all on the youngish side, which made sense. A man with a family to feed couldn't leave them to join the permanent army. He didn't recognize any of them, which meant that, at some point, his brothers and his father had peeled away. That was fine with him. It'd be a disaster to put his older brothers in a position to take orders from him.

"So." He cleared the morning rasp out of his throat. "Here we are. Last night was exciting. You joined the unit of the giant slayer. And now you wake up with a sixteen-year-old."

A few of the men chuckled. A few more studied the ground in front of them.

"I'm not the tallest or the strongest. I'm not the most experienced. But I have one thing, one thing that if we come together under its banner, we will be the greatest unit of the entire army."

David paused.

"Trust in the Lord."

He didn't let the eye rolling or sniffing of some of the men distract him but continued in as steady a tone as he could manage. "It was trust in the Lord that gave me the confidence to step forward to fight the giant. It was trust in the Lord that let me run at him with only a shepherd's sling." His words came faster and louder. "Nobody but the Lord. Our Lord. If we learn to rely on Him, then no army will be able to stand against us."

What he had to say next sounded like pride, but it was the truth. "Adonai is with me. If you are with me, I know He'll be with us."

David stood. "We'll learn how to fight hard and well; we'll learn about military strategy, and we'll learn all of it together. But without Him, we might as well be learning how to help our enemies win, because that's how much good knowledge on its own will do us." He took a deep breath. "If this doesn't sound like something you want to be a part of, go ahead and leave now."

Several men got to their feet. Some of those who remained with him mocked them.

Whatever it had done to the men, his pep talk had worked on himself. There was a lot to learn. He'd definitely make mistakes and maybe more of his unit would leave. But Adonai was with him. It didn't matter who else was against him.

"Let them go in peace. We're on the same side."

He didn't know who was crazier. The king for setting this in motion? These thirty-eight men for sticking with him?

Or his own self, for thinking he could do it?

16. Battlefield, two years later, spring 1022 bce

Saul wanted to bash the messenger's forehead in with his sword hilt. "Of course they were victorious," he said instead. "What else would they be?" He waved the messenger and everyone else out of his tent.

Making David a commander two years ago had backfired. Massively.

He'd imagined that the men would wake up after that celebration in horror that a skinny sixteen-year-old boy was their boss. They'd desert him, David would be shamed, people would laugh at him instead of love him, and he wouldn't be a danger to Saul.

As it turned out, it was considered one of his most brilliant decisions as king. Even Jonathan turned against him, taking the boy and his unit under his wing. David won every battle he entered and his division was so unified they moved and thought as one.

The more David won, the more the army respected him; the harder his unit fought, the margin of Israel's victories grew greater, as did the love the people showed him. The boy didn't realize the power he could wield with all that adulation behind him. Or, he didn't realize it yet.

It was only a matter of time before the people would ask for him to be king.

The one advantage to the whole mess was that, when some of the men followed David out two years ago, singing and dancing like the drunken fools they were, all Saul needed to do was sneer at the backs of those who followed David and the thugs who remained became loyal to him. He was biding his time with them, giving them prime plunder, the best tents, moving them first into homes. They'd repay him when the time came.

But the time was too long in coming.

It would be easier if David did anything wrong, but he was utterly blameless. Saul's hands were tied. If he tried to manufacture or invent anything treasonous, let alone ungodly, nobody would believe it. And even trying would reveal how much of a threat he thought David was to him. There had to be a way to make the boy's life unbearable and also more dangerous.

All the way back from the latest skirmish with the Ammonites, Saul clapped and cheered and tossed small plunder at villagers while thinking of ways to dishonor David. There were plenty of ways to kill David. It was fun to imagine all of them, and the men loyal to him would probably relish it, but a murdered David would make his own position more precarious, not more secure. He needed a way to dishonor David that would add honor to his own name. Or at least not taint his name.

When he got home, he'd barely washed his feet and changed from his blood-spattered battle garments when his daughter Merab accosted him.

"Father, you said you'd make a decision about who I will marry when you came back from this battle. I am nearly too old for anybody to want me. My cousins were all already married at my age and they make fun of me. I'm the king's daughter and I'm a joke. Is that what you want for your family? So what have you decided? You're home from the battle and I need to know. When? Who? I don't even care who anymore..."

Merab's harangue went on. His head pounded at the shrill edge in her voice. Whoever he married her off to would have a headache every day of his life, if not from her voice, then from her bossing. She'd be the end of whomever she married.

And there it was, standing in front of him, with kohl around her eyes and gold bands circling her arms. Merab would marry David.

She'd be out of his household and she'd be David's headache, literally. The mere idea was enough to make him want to dance, but that wasn't a seemly activity for a king, even in front of his family.

"Wipe that garbage off your face," he said. "There'll be plenty of time for that when you're married."

"But that's the problem." She didn't touch the kohl. "I'm

not married and my cousins are all having babies and doing their eyes and I'm—"

"Do it now or you don't get your surprise."

Merab pouted. "My oil is upstairs."

Any of his soldiers who gave him this much trouble over a simple order would have their beard cut off. Sometimes, war was so much easier than home. "There's oil for my spear behind me."

"Fine." Merab stomped behind the throne.

Soon she was back in front of him, clean-faced.

"If you'd let me get a word in edgewise, you'd have found out that I've decided you are to be married."

"You did? When?"

He hadn't worked that out yet, so he smiled.

"You've already arranged it, that's why you're smiling." Merab kissed his cheek. "I knew you'd come through for me. Actually, I didn't know that. I was sure you'd ignore me again. I can't wait. I have to go tell Mother and Michal. We need to start planning right away." She was already out the door.

Saul smirked. Now he got to spread the good news, too. He ordered that David be brought to him.

David bowed low when he entered the room. Not as low as he used to, but enough to be respectable. "I am honored that Adonai's Anointed wishes to see me."

Saul waved him closer. "Reports of your performance in battle were excellent, as usual, my son."

David put his right hand on his chest and dipped his head.

"Which reminds me." Saul sifted the fringe of his tassels through his fingers. "Do you remember what the reward was for the man who killed the giant, Goliath?"

"That was a long time ago, my lord."

"I'm sure you know it."

David frowned slightly and Saul drank it in. It wasn't often that David seemed unsure of how to proceed.

"Remind me." Saul lifted his chin. "Now."

"You promised that the man's family would be free from paying taxes and that he could ma- marry your daughter."

"Have they happened?"

"My father is grateful for the release of the tax obligation." David smiled. "So much so that he still sends it out of the pleasure at having enough to give as a gift for the good of Israel."

Of course honorable men came from honorable households. Irritating. "But my daughters are still unmarried."

"Children are a blessing."

In theory. "It's high time that I complete my vow. You killed the giant, so you get the girl. I am ready to give you Merab, my oldest daughter." Saul opened his arms. "Come and kiss your father-in-law."

But David didn't approach the throne. He dropped to his knees and hung his head. "Who am I, and what is my family in Israel that I should be the king's son-in-law?"

"You are a commander. A beloved warrior." Saul was impressed that he didn't choke over the word "beloved."

"I'm the youngest of eight sons in a family that has no standing, no wealth to make its way down to me."

"And I am from the smallest tribe, yet I am king."

"We are grateful that the Lord chose you."

"And now I am choosing you as my son-in-law."

David gathered his tunic into his fists. "You wish me to leave my men here and return to Bethlehem? Only to join you when you raise the tribal army?"

As good as it sounded to send David away, Saul needed to keep close tabs on him. And the army needed him. "This is a new time in Israel. You will stay here to train with your unit. Unless you are tired of army life already?"

"Oh, no, no, no, my lord. But I live in the tent city with my men. I have no house to put a wife in."

Saul stared him down.

"My lord." David was looking desperate.

"Get up." This was going beyond the customary back-and-forth refusal of a gift when both parties knew you'd accept it. "Off your knees." Saul stood two hand spans in front of David, taking full advantage of his height. Nothing was going to please him more than putting David in his place.

"David?" Jonathan walked into the room.

David took a few steps back.

"Father?"

Saul wandered to one of the windows. "I'm trying to redeem my promise that the giant slayer could marry my daughter."

Jonathan grinned. "That explains the extra noise from Mother and the girls." He slapped David's back. "You're going to be my brother-in-law. Best news of the day. Michal must be thrilled."

"Not Michal." Saul frowned. "Merab."

Jonathan eyed Saul and then burst out laughing.

"I fail to see what is funny about that," Saul said.

Jonathan wiped his eyes. "Merab doesn't know, does she?"

"She knows I've chosen a husband for her."

"Actually, that's not so funny," Jonathan said. "David is my friend."

"Are you saying you wouldn't wish your sister on him?"

"You know how Merab loves being the king's daughter. She's expecting you to marry her to a future tribal chief, someone with a status at least approaching her own. No offense, David."

"None taken," David said. "Good point."

Jonathan and David shared a private smile; Saul gritted his teeth.

"Think of it from her side," Jonathan said. "For most of his time at the fortress, he's been a servant."

Saul didn't respond.

"And now he's in the army. How is he going to keep her in linens and gold?"

Why did his children feel free to speak their minds to him? Surely other fathers didn't suffer through this.

"David, I'd like to have a private word with my father."

"But stay close," Saul said.

Jonathan waited until David left the room. "Not to mention, if you marry her to someone so far beneath her, and she stays here in Gibeah, you'll never hear the end of it. She'll complain about her plight over and over and over and at an ever increasing pitch. Why not marry her to someone from a distant tribe?"

Jonathan did have a good grasp of the situation with his sister. The idea of shipping her off as a reward for someone who helped him early in his kingship sounded better.

But that didn't solve his David issue. Saul scratched his chin through his beard. "Why did you think it was Michal?"

Jonathan snorted. "Watch her anytime David's around."

"You expect me to shadow my daughter?"

"Of course not." Jonathan adjusted the drape of his mantle. "Invite David to play for the family this week and you'll see it."

His son was free with his opinions about Merab, but for Michal, he turned diplomatic. "Or you could just tell me."

Jonathan cleared his throat. "Michal fancies herself in love with David."

Saul gave him a long look. "We do not speak about the unmarried girls of our family in that way."

"I didn't mean–. Yes, Father."

"Tell David I require his musical services tonight at family dinner. And tell him to wash the soldier off himself and wear that cloak you gave him."

If Jonathan was right, he still might be able to marry one of his daughters to David. The idea of the-one-who-does-no-wrong being harried to within a thumb span of his life had been sweet, but marriage to Michal might be even better. David would become part of the House of Saul. With another level of loyalty between them and with David's honorable nature, he'd be even less likely to have his head turned by people who wanted someone else to be king.

*****

Wash the soldier off?

What did the king mean by that? The "washing" part David got, but was he supposed to be less of a soldier? Less brave? Less strong? Being a soldier wasn't something David put on, it was what he *was*.

That afternoon, instead of working on weapon techniques with his men, David snuck to the well used mostly by field workers and beat his best tunic against the rocks. He laid it out to dry and then drew bucket after bucket of water to rinse the grime from his head. With the knots undone, his hair fell well past his shoulders.

The field workers had their heads bent to their tasks and girls from the village wouldn't come to this well in the middle of the day, so he stripped to his loincloth and scrubbed off what had to be several layers of skin.

The sun blasted his now-tender skin, but he tipped his face up and let himself bake. His hair brushed against his back. He shifted his head side to side to feel it again. When had his hair ever felt so soft? It was like newborn hair. This must be what the king meant.

But he was an officer, not a mere soldier—an officer who shouldn't be seen mostly naked, fussing with his appearance. He threw on the still-damp tunic and returned to his tent in the army camp on the other side of Gibeah.

David had never worn the fine linen cloak, although he shook it out and refolded it now and then. If it had been a real gift, given to him publicly as a reward for leading his men to victory, he could have worn it with honor. But it had always felt more like a bribe so he'd forget Saul had hurled that spear at him.

Did the king order him to wear it so he'd look marriage-able ? Or was it a not-so-subtle signal that Saul might accidentally or on purpose try to kill him if he didn't cooperate? Knowing the king, it was probably both.

The cloak made all the spots on his tunic stand out, so

he wound it tightly enough that less than a handspan of the tunic was visible. He secured it with his belt, which had been Jonathan's. It looked so disreputable next to the linen, it was like that old joke: you can dress up a goat, but you can't invite it to dinner unless it's dead.

He tugged at the hem to smooth it against his chest. The sandstorm in his stomach made small, swirling eddies that died down when he breathed deeply. He held onto his lyre with a white-knuckle grip and trudged up the hill.

The city's gate guard raised his eyebrows at David's get-up, but David didn't respond. There weren't many people on the streets, so he didn't have to field any spoken or unspoken commentary about his appearance. The fortress's gate guard frowned and stepped in front of him.

"You're late," the guard said. "They've already started."

"I wasn't told–" David broke off. He didn't owe the guard an explanation. "The king's waiting for me."

The guard clipped David's shoulder as he passed through, but he was used to those little power plays.

The courtyard was done up like it was for the New Moon Feast. The matting on the ground was fresh and clean. Blue and purple-edged banners hung from pegs high on the walls and billowed in the breeze. Even the weather was perfect, warm but not too hot with a breeze slight enough to keep things comfortable without depositing sand in the food.

The soldiers never got to see Saul's daughters. Even David, who'd spent a lot of time over the last four years at the fortress, had only gotten glimpses of them. Everything about them shimmered, from their hair, to their skin, to the scarves shot through with gold thread, and the hammered gold and bronze cuffs around their arms and ankles.

David wanted to laugh. Saul thought he was worthy to marry one of *them*? They were almost a different species of woman from his country village sisters.

One of the skills they taught scouts was how to walk silently, so he was a few steps away before they noticed him. All conversation and eating stopped. Some of the faces turned toward him were curious, others hostile, others disdainful. Only Jonathan's was friendly. The king's smile was more a stretching his lips over his teeth than a sign of welcome, which sent another gust of wind through the sandstorm inside David.

17. Doubling the requirement

David bowed his head. "It is an honor to be here."

"My family has been overhearing you play for years," Saul said, "nagging me to stop hoarding the best musician for myself."

There was the king's wife, Ahinoam. David knew Abinadab and Malkishua from the army, and Ish-Bosheth was too young to fight, but he hung around like David used to. He tried hard not to look directly at Merab and Michal.

Jonathan winked at David, which should have helped, but didn't.

Ish-Bosheth was close to David's age. Did he look so surly because David was in the army and he wasn't? He said, "That cloak looks familiar. It definitely isn't something a shepherd would wear."

Merab giggled. It wasn't a friendly sound.

Jonathan's laugh sounded forced. "It's an old one of mine."

Ish-Bosheth raised an eyebrow. Jonathan shrugged.

David stayed mute. He knew better than to get in the middle of brothers.

"Didn't you work on that one, Michal?" Ahinoam said.

Michal blushed and ducked her head. "I think so," she whispered.

Merab giggled again and pointed at David's feet. "Right there, on the hem. I can see where you messed up."

"Did not," Michal said.

"Did so." Merab waved David over without looking at him.

Because he was more a servant than a guest, he went, sending up a prayer that Adonai would save him from marrying this girl.

Merab ignored him and lifted up the offending hem. "Right there."

David tried not to be obvious about inhaling, but the king's daughters even smelled different from regular girls, like wildflowers and honey.

Michal sniffed. "So what? You were learning once, too."

"Daughters," Ahinoam said.

An uneasy silence fell.

David cleared his throat. "Do you have anything specific you'd like me to play, my lord?"

Saul didn't even look at David as he gestured for him to move back. "Stay in the background. And no words."

Not singing words was odd, but the rest of it was fine with him. Sitting in a corner and playing his lyre was something he could do with his eyes closed, so he did. As usual, joy and peace bloomed throughout his spirit while he played. He couldn't keep silent, so he sang sounds, his voice bending and sliding and adapting to his mood.

He opened his eyes a sliver to gauge whether they were enjoying the music. Michal was watching him through the curtain of her hair, out of the corner of her eyes. His skin went hot and prickly and his throat closed up. Now that he'd caught her looking at him, he couldn't stop himself from checking to see whether she still was. After the fourth time, he shifted so she wasn't in his sight line.

After a couple of hours, Saul summoned him closer. "My daughters want to hear one of your songs."

"Father," Merab whispered through clenched teeth. "I do not."

"Father wants to marry you off to him," Ish-Bosheth said in a teasing sing-song.

"What?" Merab's screech raised the hairs on the back of David's neck. "You can't be serious."

"He did kill the giant," Saul said.

She crossed her arms and glared at David and then at her father.

Saul said something like "pish," and motioned at David to get to it.

The king was clearly trying to show David to his best advantage, but David didn't think a song existed that would move Merab to see him as anything but beneath her. Which was good. Maybe if they both refused, the king would see sense.

In any case, he sang for the glory of Adonai, not to impress some girl, and that's what he'd do now.

"When I look at the night sky, I see the work of Your fingers," David sang, tipping his head back. The sky was pitch black and pierced with countless stars.

> The moon and the stars You set in place.
> Who are we that You should think of us?
> Mere humans that You should care for us?
> You madc us only a little lower than angels and
> You crowned us with glory and honor.

Michal sighed and David rushed into the next verse, and then into the next song until the small children were asleep on the mothers' laps, and the mothers leaned against their husbands' shoulders. David's men would be long asleep by now, as would everyone in the rest of Gibeah. He trailed off, and after he plucked the last note, there was complete silence.

At breakfast the next day, David stirred his food without eating it. The paleness of the yoghurt and wheat against the deep brown of the bowl reminded him of Michal, her creamy cloak next to her soft brown skin.

His second in command, Eleazar, knocked David's elbow and snickered.

"What?" David looked up.

His men were smirking at him.

"I asked you what was on the agenda today," Eleazar said.

David scrubbed his hand over his face. "King had me at the compound late."

One of the men harrumphed. "Isn't it time for the king to move us into the city?"

"We're the last ones left in the tent camp," someone else said. "Is this how the king rewards his best unit?"

They looked expectantly at David.

"Our living situation didn't come up."

There was more grumbling, but he didn't stop it this time. None of them were nomads who'd grown up living in tents. After two years' worth of promises that they'd be moving into houses in the city, his men had earned the right to complain.

But not to wallow in it.

David scarfed down his breakfast. "Today is a good day to work on our armor."

After his last growth spurt, his breastplate was too short and too tight. It rode up and exposed his belly when he raised his arms above the shoulder. The length of the kilt was fine, although he should let out the belt and add a few more straps. For the first time since joining the army two years ago, he was big enough to look like a real soldier, not a boy playing army.

When he got back to his tent, he gathered his current armor, what was left of the giant's armor, his dagger, and the pinchers he took off a Philistine raider. He sat cross-legged in the clearing in the middle of their tents. The first task was to pry apart the rest of the giant's breast-plate. He dug the tip of his dagger under the metal clips holding the leather and bronze together and twisted.

His men joined him to clean and repair their armor and weapons.

David grinned at the small pile of clips at his feet. "You know what I love?"

A few men grunted.

"I love that I'm using a Philistine double-edged iron dagger to take apart Philistine armor and rebuild it using Philistine pinchers so it'll protect me from Philistines."

They all chuckled as they bent over their work.

The bronze strips that, on the giant, went diagonally from shoulder to sternum, fit horizontally around David's torso, but not his chest anymore. The first time he expanded his breastplate for a growth spurt, he added a couple of strips to the bottom, but this would be a more extensive alteration. He wrenched off the shoulder straps and upper arm guards and sewed a handspan of new leather at the top of the armor.

He laid a bronze strip on top of the leather, overlapping the previous strip by a little bit. It was tedious work. He had to poke his dagger through the holes already in the bronze, nick the leather underneath, lift off the metal to widen the slit in the leather enough to accept a ring, thread the metal ring between the two, and then seal the ring shut with the pincher.

All the fine finger work irritated his already raw and tender skin. It had been a long time since he'd played his lyre for an entire evening. He was blowing on his fingertips when Jonathan sauntered over and indicated with his chin that the men should scram.

His men checked with him, and he nodded his permission; they moved back near Eleazar's tent.

Jonathan sat and tweaked David's beard. "It's filled out."

David kept working. Jonathan didn't usually tease him about his youth. It was one of David's favorite things about their friendship.

"That was some prime singing last night. You made me tear up and I've heard you hundreds of times before." Jonathan picked up one of the bronze strips.

David frowned. This didn't feel like a casual visit.

"Working on your armor?"

David couldn't concentrate on the fussy work, so he put the armor down and picked up his belt that used to be Jonathan's.

"I don't know how my sisters can resist you after you sang to them last night."

Not him, too. "Don't even tease me about that."

"I understand about refusing Merab, believe me. But what about Michal?"

David scooped fat from a jar and attacked the salt

stains that had showed up so clearly against the smooth linen of Jonathan's cloak. "The king hasn't offered Michal."

Jonathan nudged David. "But she's a better option, eh?"

It wasn't a joking matter.

"Come on. This is me you're talking to."

David threw the belt onto his lap.

Jonathan picked up one end of it. "You're closer to me than any of my brothers." All the false humor was gone. "For you to actually *be* my brother–" His voice broke.

David scraped at some dirt with the tip of his dagger. "A poor shepherd doesn't marry a king's daughter."

"You're not a poor shepherd anymore."

"That's all I have to look forward to when I get too old for the army. No matter what I do here, when I go back to Bethlehem, I'll always be the youngest son."

"So don't leave the army."

"And bring her to live here?" David jabbed his thumb at his tent.

Jonathan scoffed. "Come on. My father will give you a house. You're overdue for one, anyway."

"Message delivered."

Jonathan tugged on his end of the belt until David looked at him. "I'm not only doing my father's bidding. I need a friend in my family. I want a brother who isn't constantly competing with me for the throne. We could start to build our dynasty. Me as king and you as commander of the army. We'd be greater even than my father and Abner and you know it."

David's resolve melted a bit. "I told my nephew you were the brother I never had, although I already had too many brothers." But he still couldn't wrap his thoughts around it. "Do you think it worked better to have more of the army divided into raiding parties?"

"Consider it." Jonathan tossed the belt back in David's lap before lowering his head and drawing in the sand with his finger.

Would Jonathan drop the subject? Or was he stalling before hitting David with another argument? David could hear Eliab's mocking "Mr. High and Mighty" for even allowing himself to entertain it.

Jonathan edged back and David saw that he'd been working on a battle diagram. David stifled a relieved sigh.

"We barely held the front line," Jonathan said. "Next time we have to reduce the raiding parties a bit to make the front stronger."

Now that they were talking strategy, his men drifted back. "So long as we still get to be on a raiding party," one of them said. "Nobody can argue with our success." The rest laughed and said variations of "Oh yeah."

"Jonathan's right, though," David said. "We lost too many men from the front lines." He drew a cluster of short lines at the back of the Israelite group, and then another at the front. "I say we beef up the rank of slingers and put them in the front *and* in the back. The ones in the front could keep the enemy from advancing so far so quickly, or at least give them something else to worry about. They can't be as focused with the sword if they have to worry about all the rocks flying."

"You could lead that rank, you know," Jonathan said.

"We're not putting David in the back." Abner's growl startled them and everyone but Jonathan scrambled to their feet.

"So, you think we were weak on the front, do you?" Abner peered at several men in turn, his thick eyebrows making him look furious.

David lifted his chin, daring the commander to ignore the truth.

"Well, you're right," Abner said.

The soldiers exhaled audibly.

"But it's a tough one." Abner crouched and added his own marks to the diagram. "The raiding parties are always what win us the battle. So we have to balance our surprise attack," he traced wide loops from the Israelite side to behind the enemy line, "with just enough men at the front to be respectable."

"What about David's slingers idea?" Jonathan asked.

Abner wiped out the front slinger lines with his thumb. "Men don't want to be only slingers. They want to be in the thick of the action. Besides, once we have an active engagement, their stones are as likely to hit one of our own."

David frowned. "The slingers hang back the entire time?"

"They have daggers or axes for anyone who makes it through the infantry," Abner said. "But if someone can handle a sword or a spear, we take them for the front."

"That could be yet another element of surprise, then." David knelt and slashed deep lines through the sand from the back slingers to the center of the battle. "Some slingers in the front to pick off their front line, but give the slingers other weapons training. If the enemy doesn't know a second line of seriously trained men are coming, the slingers could clean up and we could have as great a victory at the front as we do on the raids."

"The slingers are our last line of defense." Abner sat back on his heels. "Using them in offense leaves the camp unprotected and *we'd* be vulnerable to raiding parties."

Jonathan piled up some sand. "Too bad they haven't tried the one champion gambit again." He smashed the pile with his fist.

A number of men slapped David on the back. He rose quickly so nobody was tempted to ruffle his hair. They generally deferred to him without regard for his age, but every now and then, they'd make him feel like a kid, which undermined his command.

"You've given me something to think about, though." Abner stood. "Now let me give you something to ponder."

Not him, too. David crossed his arms and returned Abner's level gaze.

"We all have such respect for you." Abner egged on David's men, who agreed loudly and enthusiastically. "And this hasn't gone unnoticed by the king." He smiled and spread his hands open. "In fact, the king truly likes you."

Maybe he did, once, but that wasn't true anymore. "I'm honored that Adonai's Anointed has noticed the work my men and I do."

Abner ignored that and addressed the soldiers. "What would you say if I told you that your commander had the chance to be the king's son-in-law but turned him down?"

Great. Now Abner was going to use his men against him. Why did the king want this marriage so badly?

"And move to the fortress?" one of the men asked.

David reared back. Doing everything together was one of the keys to their success, which made for one more reason he couldn't marry Michal. "I need to be with my men."

"Sir," Eleazar said. "It *is* a great honor."

"Think of the influence," another man said.

"Your increase in stature would be good for us," Eleazar said. "We might all get to move inside the walls."

Of all the justifications so far, that one went the farthest. If marriage to Michal would benefit his men, he had to consider it.

"There's still the problem of the bride price." David dangled his belt between two fingers. "Here, my lord the king, have this stained belt that was already used when it was given to me."

A number of men laughed.

"That is your final objection?" Abner asked. "The bride price?"

"It's the objection that can't be argued away," David said.

Abner took a step closer. "But if somehow it were?"

David opened his mouth, but Abner put his hand up. "Don't rush your answer."

He'd be Jonathan's brother in truth, Michal was beautiful and seemed sweeter than her sister, and he could make sure his men would benefit. But the son-in-law of the king?

Thinking about it wasn't helping.

Adonai, he prayed. *You've already given me a life I never imagined. To be married to a daughter of the king is so far above me, but if You are determined to give me this blessing, I'll figure out how to use it for Your glory.*

David waited. No voice came, telling him what to do, but his heart stopped racing, which was as good a sign as any. "If my men are behind me, the king wants it, and his eldest son is for me, I'd be a fool to refuse."

Jonathan leapt up and put David in a friendly headlock.

Abner clapped his hands as loud as a whip crack. "I was hoping you'd say that. What King Saul wants and needs more than jewels or gold or fine clothing is vengeance against our enemies."

The men nodded.

"All the king wants is one hundred Philistine foreskins."

David blinked. That was an oddly specific thing.

Abner shouted to the men, "You'd do that for your commander, wouldn't you?"

The men roared their agreement.

If his men were eager to head out again, who was David to throw cold water on them? The Lord kept opening this tent flap, and he wasn't about to keep refusing to walk through it.

David spun his belt around over their heads while his men cheered. If that were truly all the king required, then David would double it.

*****

Gibeah. Two moons later, early summer 1022 bce

Saul's skin was still crawling. No matter how often he washed himself, no matter how much oil he rubbed on himself, no matter how fine the linen clothes he put on, he itched like he was infested with bugs.

Was it only a week ago that he'd stood at the main gate

and watched David's men carry him into Gibeah on their shoulders, that sack held high in David's hand?

A violent shiver ran across him. That sack. He squeezed his eyes shut, but it wasn't enough to banish the image of it on the floor, two hundred Philistine foreskins spilling out of it. If he hadn't come up with, "And that's how I feel about my enemies," after throwing up in front of everyone, it would have been the beginning of the end of his kingship, for sure.

Today, during the wedding celebration, every time he looked at David, he saw those bits of dried and bloody skin. Every time he looked at his beautiful, pure daughter, he saw David's hands on the Philistines' members and imagined him putting those same hands on Michal. The images made sleep impossible.

"He was supposed to be killed!"

Two servants scurried into the room and asked whether he needed anything.

Saul frowned. Had he bawled those words aloud?

He waved them away.

This should have been the happiest time of his life. Merab was far north in Meholah, married to Adriel. Despite her presence, the tribal leaders of Issachar were sending more tributes than ever. Michal was married to a hero. His sons were starting to have sons of their own, although Jonathan didn't yet. But Saul lay awake every night, plagued by bugs he couldn't see.

David had to die.

He was the root of all Saul's problems. The people loved him too much. The only death they'd accept was if he was killed in battle, but he was too good. His luck had to run out eventually, especially if someone made sure he pushed that luck.

"Servants!" When they ran back in, he whispered, "Take a lamp and fetch Abner. Do not alert any member of my household, or of his, or I will have you killed."

After they left, Saul rubbed olive oil into his scalp and his beard. It was so warm and soothing, but the effect only lasted until he moved to the next spot. Finally, Abner stood before him.

Saul held a lamp up. "Cousin, can I trust you?"

"Is that you, Saul?" Abner made a show of peering at him. "Or is it an imposter?"

"Of course it's me." Saul put the oil pot down. "I need to trust someone. I can't bear this burden on my own."

"I've faithfully served you for thirty years and led your army for twenty-eight. I've never hesitated to do your bidding–"

Saul snorted.

"If I've done anything to offend you, tell me and I will give you justice."

"It was your job to help me enforce my decree that nobody could eat until we defeated the Philistines."

Abner frowned. "You're still hung up on that? That was at least a dozen campaigns ago."

"You should've supported me. Instead, you convinced me not to kill the one man who ate in violation of my direct order."

"But it was Jonathan."

"It was my vow." Saul's blood boiled hotter with each word.

"Let me speak as the cousin who raced over these hills with you when we were children. Will you allow me that?"

Saul shrugged.

"Jonathan is the best of your sons. The bravest, the boldest, the most beloved. I didn't want you to be known as the king who killed his own son."

Saul stared at Abner without blinking until his eyes stung. "Was it just Jonathan, or do you object to killing heroes in general?"

"Other than that one time, for one who was my own blood and yours, have I ever denied you anything?"

No, he had not. "So if I were to ask you to–"

"If you've lost that much confidence in my abilities, take your spear and run me through." Abner stood with his arms out to the sides, leaving himself utterly open. "If I had my sword on me, I'd ask you to hold it so I could fall on it. I'd rather do that than listen to you question my loyalty."

"Put your arms down."

"What do you want?"

Saul's fingers tangled themselves back in his beard before he realized what he was doing and jerked them out. "When we go out against the Philistines, the Ammonites, the Amalekites, whoever's next, I want you to give my new son-in-law and his men the most dangerous assignments."

"They're my best men for those jobs."

"That's not what I mean. I'm talking about insane assignments. I want him at the front of every line, leading every raiding party, spying deep in enemy territory."

"My lord." Abner's voice was almost too kind. "He already is."

Bile boiled up from Saul's stomach, but he breathed deeply and forced it back down. "What village of ours is constantly under attack?"

Abner thought. "Lachish. They've got the Philistines to the east, Amalekites to the south, plus everyone else who wants to control the gateway to the northern and western trade routes."

"That giant a few years ago," Saul said. "Where was he from?"

"Gath."

"Isn't Lachish also near Gath?"

Abner frowned a bit and then nodded.

Saul raised his eyebrows. "They despise David in Gath."

A muscle pulsed in Abner's jaw.

"Send him and his men to Lachish," Saul said. "To protect it, of course. A year should do it."

"He was married yesterday," Abner said. "When–"

"By the end of the day." Once the Philistines found out that the boy who'd killed their giant and slaughtered so many of their soldiers was close by, they'd fall over themselves at the chance to kill him. It was almost enough to make Saul smile.

Saul dismissed Abner and returned to his throne. He could picture David's men carrying his lifeless body, the face contorted at the pain of the wounds the Philistines would inflict.

Saul poured more oil on his hand and massaged it into his scalp by his right ear.

Even better, by now, David would be such a prize that the Philistines would keep the body after killing him. They'd need to exact their revenge. Maybe they'd cut off his head and march around with it on a spear, leaving his body to be eaten by dogs and birds and other dirty scavengers.

Saul twisted a hank of his hair until it tugged at his scalp.

David's men would come back to Gibeah with their tunics torn and dirt on their heads, and no music would be able to soothe the grief of the people because their perfect hero was jeered at by their enemies, his body spread over the fields and residing in the stomachs of wild animals, never to be recovered.

A twinge of pain startled him. He lowered his hand. Coarse black hair curled around his fingers, and when he tested that area of his head with his other hand, his fingertips came away spotted with blood. At least that spot didn't itch anymore. He shoved the hair into a crack between the stones of his throne and wiped off his hands.

He had time to break his fast before Michal stormed in to complain about him taking her husband away.

18. Road outside Gibeah. Two years later, early spring 1020 BCE

David told his right foot to move ahead, but it wouldn't. He stared at his left foot, but it was stuck to the road as if a stake held it there. Lifting his head took the same amount of effort as pulling that donkey out of the mudslide two days ago. He could see Gibeah, but he could also see the hill.

His men were the same: slumped shoulders, hung heads, and closed eyes. He wasn't the only one too tired to move on.

"Men." David cleared his throat and swallowed hard. "Men! We'll camp here tonight and finish our journey tomorrow so we can return like the champions we are."

There were no cheers, just the thud of packs hitting the ground.

David stood over his pile of skins and sticks, staring at it without seeing it. How was he going to put a tent up when he could barely move his arms? He couldn't ask his men to do it for him. They were as exhausted as he.

He closed his eyes and, at first, soundlessly moved his lips, but eventually his voice gained in volume.

If Adonai had not been on our side,
  We would have been swallowed alive.
  The waters would've engulfed us,
  A torrent would have overwhelmed us.

His voice had never been worse. In fact, he sounded like that donkey. But he kept going, and as he sang, he crouched and untied the tent.

O, my Strength, to You I sing praises,
  For You, my God, are my refuge.
  Your unfailing love gives me strength.

He had to stop singing to grunt while he pushed himself upright. The key was not to think about the whole job, but to sing and do things one step at a time. When the tent was half up, word filtered to him that a group was coming down from Gibeah. From this distance, he couldn't tell who they were, or even how many.

"Ignore them," David called out. He didn't care whether it was King Saul himself. He and his men needed rest, and they were taking it. The added pressure of visitors gave David a boost of energy and he finished his set-up.

Judging by the snores buzzing through the air when the group from the city reached them, most of his men were asleep. David stood outside his tent, swaying.

It was Jonathan. David didn't have to appear strong for him, so he collapsed.

Jonathan struggled to lift him into a sitting position. "Is this really David, my brother?"

"Only a shadow of him."

"When did you last eat?" Jonathan didn't wait for an answer, but waved one of his men forward. "I seem to be too late for the men, but here you go."

Jonathan piled bread and cheese and raisin cakes into a bowl, which he placed in David's lap. It wasn't until Jonathan filled a cup with wine and held it to David's mouth as if he were a baby being weaned that David snapped out of his stupor.

He gulped the liquid. It hurt going down and his body immediately threatened to reject it. He tipped his head back and breathed deeply. When the wine didn't come up, he tried the food, slowly at first, but eventually setting on it like a lion on her first fat spring kill.

Meanwhile, Jonathan went from tent to tent, feeding anyone who was awake.

Tears stung David's eyes. "How can I ever repay you?"

"You're my brother." Jonathan sat on his right and put his hand on David's shoulder. "Will I sound like an old mother if I confess that I've been worried sick since the rains started last week? It was terrible timing for my father to order you back."

That was an understatement. The end-of-season rains seemed even heavier than usual this year. David put his left hand over Jonathan's hand. "You are truly the Lord's instrument tonight."

They sat like that for several slow breaths until David patted Jonathan's hand and crawled into his tent.

Jonathan followed him in. "Normally, I'd give you my pillow and tuck your cloak around you, but tonight, we have to talk." He lowered his voice. "There are ... developments in Gibeah you need to be aware of."

When the tent flap was securely closed, Jonathan continued. "It's my father. When you sent your latest report from Lachish, he went... He got..."

"What?"

"He wants to kill you."

David blinked. Had he heard that right? "Kill me?"

Jonathan nodded.

David was too exhausted to regulate himself. "Why? Because thanks to my men Lachish is thriving? Because they were able to complete their harvest and thresh it, in full, two years in a row? I lost ten men there. Ten. Their bones sent back to their fathers in shrouds." Hot blood coursed through his veins. "I'm not boasting, but the facts are that we've been decisive in ensuring victory for Israel."

"More so than any other unit," Jonathan murmured.

"What have I done to deserve death?"

"Succeeded."

"So I should dishonor the Lord and Israel and my father

and my men and the king by trying to lose now and then?" David's breathing was loud in the tent.

"I have a plan," Jonathan said. "I know my father. He just needs to listen to a reasonable person."

Jonathan told him the plan; given that David wasn't calm enough to come up with an alternative, he agreed.

"I know you're anxious to get home."

"I've been gone for two years. I spent only one night with my wife."

"Trust me. Michal brings that up all the time."

David swallowed. It was so long ago. He barely remembered what she looked like. "How is she?"

"She's turned into Merab, nagging Father to let you stay in Gibeah long enough for her to have a son."

David knew what his sister Abigail went through before Amasa came along. "Other women are mocking her?"

"Not so much after she got Father to send their husbands to the front line and they were killed." Jonathan lay down and David couldn't see his face anymore.

David didn't think he'd be able to sleep after all that, but he must have, because next thing he knew, the morning sun was lighting up his tent and he could hear his men packing up.

As planned, he walked with everyone for an hour, gradually lagging behind. When he was a dozen paces back, he veered off into a field and sat at the base of the tree Jonathan pointed out. It would take Jonathan some time to lure his father here, if he even could, so David rested his head and listened to the gentle rustling of the breeze through the barley fields.

When he woke, the sun was in the center of the sky. He shook the ants off his cloak and ate the food left from last night. There was nothing to do but stay there until the plan either succeeded or Jonathan came alone to offer him protection. He was dozing off again, half aware of his surroundings, when he heard voices.

"See, Father. I told you it'd be good to get outside the walls for a reason other than going to battle."

"Hmph. The sun is center high. Get me to some shade."

The warrior in David wanted to leap up and confront the king, but he slid himself down the trunk until he was nestled in the lush grasses and wildflowers. For the first time in a week, he was grateful for the heavier than usual spring rains.

They sat under a pomegranate tree so close that he could hear the king panting.

"You didn't drag me out here for a mere stroll," Saul said.

Jonathan chuckled. "I never could fool you, Father."

"That's right."

"It's about David."

Saul's hand sliced through the heads of a patch of daisies. "You are finally going to act like my son and do what I asked you?"

"No."

"Then we're done. If you won't do it, one of my true servants will."

"Please tell me you haven't ordered your servants to kill him."

Saul sniffed.

David's hand went automatically to his hip, but his sword wasn't there. He was beginning to regret this plan of Jonathan's.

"I'm your oldest son." Jonathan paused. "The one you share the burdens of your rule with. Please hear me out."

Saul sucked his breath through his teeth. "On behalf of that shepherd?"

"He's not a shepherd. He's the best leader you've got."

"Don't remind me." Saul's words rung out like a sword striking a stone.

Jonathan lowered his voice. "If you sin against David, I'm worried that would be the end of our house."

"What have you heard? Who stands against me?"

"Nobody is standing against you. Nobody. But I see the delegations come, still testing you, still undecided about whether they trust their king."

"You're full of pleasant talk today." Saul spoke with frightening calm. "By all means, keep going."

"I trust you to follow the course of wisdom."

Saul harrumphed.

Jonathan continued, "David has never done one thing

to harm you. He's served you in every way you asked. He's soothed your spirit. He's led your men to victory. Remember that skinny boy with prickles for a beard who risked his life to kill the Philistine giant? Remember the victory the Lord gave us? The thrill of running down the enemy and slaying them left and right?"

"I remember," Saul said. "And so do all those delegations. They could easily throw their support behind David instead of me."

"Who bows the lowest to you?"

"David," Saul mumbled.

"What does he call you more often than anyone else?"

Saul grumbled.

"I know you've noticed this."

There was a long silence before Saul answered. "Did you know he was anointed by Samuel, too?"

David covered his mouth with his hand, his fingertips digging into his cheeks to keep from gasping. How did the king know about that? How long had he known?

Jonathan sounded too casual. "I'd heard something about that."

"I bet he boasts about it all the time."

It took all David's willpower not to jump up and deny it.

"Actually," Jonathan said, "he won't talk about it. To anyone."

"But you see now why David is a threat," Saul said.

"No." Jonathan's respectful tone was slipping. "So David

was anointed. Think of all the things he's done since then. Things he shouldn't have been able to do. And all in the service of who? The king. You. Maybe the Lord was preparing him to serve you. Which he has. With nothing but honor."

The king was silent. Tears pricked behind David's eyes.

"Does anyone love the Lord more than David?"

Saul pulled up a clump of grass. "That's the problem. The Lord is for him and against me."

David shut his eyes tight. It always came back to this.

"How could the Lord be against you?" Grasses crunched under Jonathan as he shifted. "You have military success that approaches Joshua's. Victories against every land that surrounds us: Moab, Ammon, Edom, Zobah, Philistia, Amalek. Your riches surpass any tribal chief. You have many sons, the command of thousands. You follow the feast days, you bring lambs and oxen and grain for sacrifice, and give offerings of plunder to the Lord. By any measure, you are blessed."

"Then why won't Samuel join me anymore?"

Jonathan stammered. "You do everything that is expected of you by our customs."

Saul was silent, as if considering it. "Maybe, but *He* isn't helping me govern this stiff-necked people."

David scrubbed his forehead. This wasn't going well.

"Is David stiff-necked?"

Saul mumbled something.

"Other than refusing to marry Merab, which nobody can blame him for, has he ever turned you down? Has he done or said anything or even given you a look to suggest that he is anything other than loyal to you? Murdering an innocent man will not put you right again. Haven't you missed his playing? His singing?"

Saul remained silent.

"Close your eyes. Humor me." Jonathan spoke in hushed tones. "Imagine this. Tribal leaders from Manasseh come to David and whisper in his ear that he should be king. Knowing what you know of David, what do you think he'd do?"

"Draw his sword and threaten to kill them."

Hope sparked in David's chest.

Jonathan gave a forced laugh. "See. You know him. Welcome him home with open arms, not with a dagger."

Saul sighed.

The king couldn't admit that David was nothing but loyal to him and still want to kill him, could he?

There was rustling, and then David could see Saul standing. "As surely as the Lord lives, David will not be killed."

"And you'll make sure all your guards and all your servants and all my brothers know this?"

There was a thick silence. David clenched his fists.

The king must have indicated that he would, because Jonathan said, "Thank you," before calling out, "David!"

Jonathan sounded more certain of Saul's state of mind than David was, but he pushed himself up on one knee. "My lord and my king."

Saul didn't look surprised. He stared first at David and then at his son. "Is this a trick?"

David put his hands up to show he wasn't reaching for a weapon.

"Father, you told me to start taking on more responsibility for our nation. Bringing you and David back together–"

Saul made a sharp slicing gesture with his right hand. "Don't speak of it. Not another word."

Jonathan held his arms out to both of them. Burrs tugged at David's ankles as he shuffled forward and let Jonathan draw them into an awkward embrace.

"Let's head back," Saul said. "Jonathan, my right hand, and David, my shield, as it should be."

David would have been more reassured if those words had been spoken with any warmth, but it was better than a dagger to the throat.

"And everything will get back to normal," Jonathan said.

On the surface, life was as it should be, but nothing was normal.

David lived with Michal in a house inside the city walls instead of in a tent in the middle of his men. Although they'd been married for two years, they'd only lived together for one night before David was sent to Lachish. So it took some adjusting.

It was also expected for him to attend feasts with Saul's family, and to be trotted out for visiting tribal delegations. He still trained with his men every day, but that was all: no eating together, no end of the evening relaxing together. The "one mind" thing that served them so well in battle was slipping.

Saul was all smiles when he saw David, but they were too hearty, too much for show. The king didn't smile at anyone else all the time, not even his own sons.

David was always aware of that conversation in the field. There was no way Saul could have simply forgotten that David had been anointed or been argued out of his conviction that the Lord was for David but not for him. They were fuel to the fire of bitterness Saul already had against both the Lord and Samuel.

He played for Saul now and then, but it never went as well as it used to.

At least once a day, Jonathan said, "Isn't it great that things are back to normal?" To which David said, "Thanks to you." And then Jonathan said, "All I had to do was remind my father how much he loved you."

Maybe even because of the constant reassurance, David was never convinced that the brokered peace would hold.

19. The second spear

When war broke out at the beginning of the dry season, it was a relief. Battle was something David understood. It was simple and it was direct.

The Philistines had barreled through Timnah and were rolling toward Beth-shemesh. The king's speeches were stirring, but when would they do more than merely stop the Philistines? Why not try to take back Timnah and so decimate and demoralize the enemy that they'd think twice before attacking the people of God?

The Philistines were ready for them, arrayed neatly in a valley and on the two flanking hills, one of which overlooked the Sorek River. They were learning. With that formation, it would be impossible to run raiding parties around the back and catch them off guard.

The Israelite commanders gathered to discuss strategy. David listened as each officer gave the same advice as always. Even Jonathan said what he always did.

But instead of agreeing with Jonathan, as he'd done every battle before this, he cleared his throat and spoke. "They've taken away the option for a sneak attack, so this time, the way to surprise them is to go straight at them, right now. Don't set up camp. Don't wait until tomorrow morning. We walk calmly down the hill in full daylight, straight at them, casual at first, but then run. They won't expect it and they won't be ready for us."

There was some hemming and hawing.

David added, "My men and I did this when we were protecting Lachish. I've seen it work on a smaller scale. I know the Lord will bless it on a larger scale."

"If you've done it before, then you lead the charge," Abner said.

"Gladly." David saw a look pass between Abner and Saul, but he didn't care what their game was, nor whether he'd played into their hands. As he was turning away to lead his men to the front of the army, he caught a hurt look on Jonathan's face, but there was no time to deal with it.

They marched down the hill in full view of the Philistine army. None of the Israelites took out their weapons, the slingers didn't hang back or to the side, the archers didn't take out or aim their bows, and nobody raised their javelin or spear. Their body armor was on, but not their helmets. They acted as if they were going to set up camp near the bottom of the hill, as usual.

When the hill started to flatten out and he was on level ground, David could feel the coiled energy and power of the army behind him, waiting for his signal, but he kept walking. He even told a joke and his men laughed and told it to the men behind them. Laughter rolled through the ranks behind him, which sounded eerier and more threatening than a battle cry.

When the Philistine army got quiet, and they were starting to figure out that something out of the ordinary was happening but didn't yet know what it was, David put on his helmet. He didn't make a big show of it, but as soon as the men around him saw the gold-plated stripe running down the center of his head, over his neck, to his shoulders, they put on their helmets, took out their weapons, and tore straight at the enemy.

His men were the first to engage. They slashed their way through what passed for the enemy front line as if it were fresh cheese. Before the rest of the Israelites even got the chance to get into the action, the Philistines turned tail and ran.

The enemy was in total confusion: the soldiers closest to the onslaught were trying to escape, but the soldiers behind them didn't yet know the fury they were about to face and pushed their comrades forwards. David and his men kept coming, and then the other Israelites arrived and it was the Goliath battle all over again.

They slaughtered the Philistines all the way back to Ekron.

After all the Philistine soldiers were either dead or escaped, there was still life in David's legs, in his arms. He could have fought more. Instead of heading back with the others, David stood with his hands on his hips and scowled at the walled city.

Someday, the people of God wouldn't be subject to

annual invasions. Hopefully when Jonathan was king, he'd be faithful enough that Adonai would give him the vision and the strength for a lasting victory. A victory that led to peace.

Everyone wanted to thump him on the back that night. Half the men called him a brilliant strategist, the other half, crazy.

Late into the evening, Jonathan came to his fire. "I got tired of waiting for you."

David stared at the flames as if mesmerized, even though he wasn't. "I didn't think your father would be happy to see me."

Jonathan shifted his head as if he had a crick in his neck. "That was some strategy."

"We can't use it on the Philistines again, but I bet our northern enemies would fall for it."

"Has something changed between us?"

"What?" David turned a puzzled look to his best friend. "No." He hoped he sounded convincing.

"Usually we discuss strategy and present it together."

"It came up when I saw how the enemy was arranged. I didn't mean to overstep."

"No, no."

David heard the implied, "not yet."

Jonathan threw the rest of his wine into the fire. "I was just ... surprised. And you know how my father talks."

David lowered his voice. "So he wants to kill me?"

"No, but he is trying to convince me that you're coming after me, trying to put yourself above me."

"And I just played into his hands." David drained his cup.

"I don't believe him," Jonathan said. "But it'd be easier for both of us if we were a united front."

David made a noncommittal noise. "I'm beat."

Jonathan left and David wrapped himself in his rough soldier's cloak. *This* was where he belonged, sleeping on the hard ground with his men, fresh from a victory Adonai gave them.

It is you.

The Voice made the inside of his head tickle. David stuck his index fingers in his ears and wiggled.

"Adonai," he muttered so nobody would hear his actual words, "I wish I knew what was me, but I give up trying to figure it out. Whatever it is, I'll do it."

Three days after the battle, David was outside the city, working with his men on using multiple weapons at the same time, when he heard shuffling feet and a thud of bodies running into each other. That wasn't part of this training. And his men didn't break out into random fights. At least, they shouldn't. He turned around, expecting to administer a reprimand.

There was Carmi, the king's household manager, flat on

his back with Eleazar looming over him, sword drawn and his knee on the older man's chest.

After all these weeks of relative peace, would the king send Carmi to kill him? It'd be a good strategy. David would never suspect his old boss and friend.

Carmi pushed at Eleazar. "What are you doing? Get off me, you goat. I have a message from the fortress for your commander."

Eleazar didn't budge. "As soon as we search you for weapons." One of David's other guards patted down Carmi, releasing him only when they were satisfied.

Carmi scrambled up, muttering about indignities as he brushed off his tunic.

David hung back until Eleazar and Amram were at his sides.

"Now." Carmi snapped at him as if he were still thirteen. "I need a word with you. Privately."

Not a chance. David hadn't gone anywhere without his guards since they'd returned from battle.

"I said privately," Carmi said.

"Not an option," Eleazar growled.

Carmi tried to grab David's arm but Amram blocked him. "What is the meaning of this?"

David let his face and voice communicate regret. "You know why."

"The king canceled those orders."

"I'm brave, not stupid, Carmi," David said.

“Remember when I could’ve cuffed you behind the head for speaking to me that way?”

“I remember.” David rested his hand on his sword hilt. “Why have you interrupted our training?”

Carmi shifted his gaze to David’s ear. “The king. He’s in a bad way.”

“Did he send for me?”

“Yes.”

There was something in his tone, so David stared him down.

“That is, no. But he needs you. Please come.”

“Why exactly does the king need me?”

“It’s the,” Carmi leaned in and whispered, “evil spirit again, but worse. So much worse. Nothing will calm him and he wants nobody.”

“So the king is in a rage and he doesn’t want anybody, yet you came to get me? Are you trying to get me killed?”

Carmi huffed. “We’re desperate, but I get it. You’ve so moved up in the world that you won’t remember the servant who taught you everything you needed to know about life in the fortress.”

“If it were a matter of playing for you because you were in a bad way, or protecting your family from bandits, I’d be there in a heartbeat.” There was no way to satisfy everyone. David wanted to help Carmi. He even wanted to help Saul. But he couldn’t do either of those things if he were dead. “I’m sorry.”

He'd barely started working with the men again when they told him someone else was coming. He muttered a curse. It was Michal's personal servant with David's lyre.

The servant held his instrument out to him and kept her gaze on the ground. "My lord, my lady sent me. Her father is not well. She begs you, the husband of her heart, to have mercy on the king and the household and play for him and let your music soothe him as it always does."

David's exhale puffed out his cheeks. That request he couldn't refuse, even though his music did not, in fact, always calm the king. Sometimes it agitated him more. But he couldn't ignore a direct request from his wife.

I am trusting you, Adonai. You are my rock of safety. Protect me.

He ordered the bulk of men to take a water break and trudged up the hill.

"My lord?" asked Eleazar.

"Stay close," David said. "Even while I'm playing. Eleazar, watch the king's throwing arm. Amram, guard the door."

It looked like half the fortress's household hovered in the courtyard, including Michal. They parted for him as if he were Moses and they were the sea. When he got to the receiving room, what he saw drew him up short.

Usually, when the king needed music, he was lethargic and barely moving, his head back against the wall, his eyes closed. Today, he couldn't keep still. His fingers convulsed. His eyes were wide open and unfocused. He was like a desert lunatic, talking gibberish. The room smelled like animal stalls that hadn't been mucked out in ages—earthy, sour, and sharp.

All of David's instincts told him to run.

Michal put her hand in the middle of his back and pushed. "We don't know what else to do."

He didn't budge.

It wasn't clear that Saul was aware of his surroundings. Whether David was able to do it or not, the king needed help. "If he's not calmer within three songs, send for the high priest."

She nodded and gave him another shove.

The king was acting like a cornered wild animal, so David treated him as such—no sudden movements, no prolonged eye contact. He slid a few steps into the room and whispered, "Adonai, you've kept me safe me before. Save me now."

That wasn't what he meant to pray. He'd meant to pray for Saul, for the evil spirit to leave him, for Adonai to bless David's music.

David strummed quietly. Maybe the music would affect the king before he realized it: a stealth raid on the evil spirit.

Two songs in and there was no change. David played gradually louder, but the king still writhed as if hornets were buzzing under his clothes.

"Sing 'Death of the Son,'" someone whispered from the doorway. "No, the 'Lilies of the Field,'" someone else said.

David glanced back to tell them to be quiet, but then their eyes widened and David whipped his head around. Saul was slumped over the side of this throne, holding his spear. Eleazar took a step towards David and then it was like time slowed down. In one smooth motion, Saul tossed the spear in the air, stood, caught it in a throwing grip and hurled it at David.

David dove to the left and heard the spear connect first with Eleazar's shield and then the wall. He glanced up. The entire spearhead was buried in the plaster.

The only sound was David and Saul's heavy breathing, the only movement was the wooden handle waving up and down.

But then Saul growled low in his throat, and Eleazar pulled David up. They ran, shouldering through the stunned crowd. The king screamed as if he were in agony. The cry rolled up David's spine and he twisted his head to get the shivery sensation off his neck.

They sprinted to his house. David went inside, but Eleazar and Amram stationed themselves on either side of the door. "What are you going to do? Fight against our own countrymen?" He shook his head. "Go back to the training field. And don't rile up the men. I don't want to make this any worse."

"But, my lord–"

"No." David put more command in his voice than he was feeling. "He's done this before and things calmed down. If we keep everything as normal as possible, there's a chance things won't escalate and I can go back to Bethlehem quietly."

Eleazar and Amram looked mutinous, but they were good soldiers. They followed orders and left him.

Michal arrived home and threw herself in his arms. "I can't believe he did that. Mother tried to tell me it was an accident, that Father was out of his mind, but I could see his eyes. He knew what he was doing." She squeezed David's rib cage. "He meant to kill you."

"I'm tough to kill." Although she clearly needed comforting, he was in command mode, and managed only to vaguely pat her back while his mind worked. "Jonathan is probably still in Naphtali?"

Michal nodded her head against his shoulder.

With him gone, David had no allies with access to the king. Then again, Jonathan would probably try to negotiate another peace, and David's faith in Saul's promises was dead.

That left his wife. "Will you do something for me?"

"Anything."

"Go to your father's house. Don't talk to him, but see..." Could he tell his wife the truth about his relationship with her father?

"See what?"

“See whether he’s issued a standing order to kill me.”

“He can’t!”

“He has before.”

“Nobody told me!”

He kissed her hair. “Jonathan kept him from following through.”

“But now he’s gone.” Michal was sobbing now.

“Just go and see. I– *we* need to know.”

She dried her tears on his tunic, kissed his jaw, and left.

Saul had tried to kill him in front of witnesses, so his time in the army was over. He’d have to leave Gibeah and return to Bethlehem. Go from leading men to herding sheep. Life as the wife of the youngest son was going to be an unpleasant shock for Michal, but her father was leaving them no choice. The question was how soon he’d have to go.

It was too quiet.

Normally, the courtyard would be full of women cooking stew and baking bread and exchanging gossip, but he heard none of that. He went to the door. The yard was empty except for two soldiers staring directly at David’s house. Saul’s thugs. One of whom winked at him.

David dashed up the ladder and skirted the edge until he reached the front room. He assumed a defensive position with his back on the wall and his sword at the ready. Now and then, he angled his head slightly to check out the window. The two men never moved.

Soon after that, Michal returned, calling his name in a hoarse whisper. The top of the ladder shook as she climbed it.

As soon as she spotted him, she crumpled into a ball on the floor. "I thought I was too late."

He kept low and dragged them both to the side of the room, well away from anything that might be shot through the window.

Her breath hitched. "I heard my father order Abner to send a dozen men to take you in the morning. He, he, he laughed and said you could have one more night with his slu–"

"Shh." David put his hand on her head and peered out the window. Indeed, ten more men made it a dozen.

Michal clung to him. "If you don't get away tonight, you'll be dead by morning."

He leaned his head back against the wall. "If they hadn't been watching the door all day, we could dress me up like a woman and I could walk right past them. I think I'd make a very attractive female."

Her eyes filled with tears. "How can you joke at a time like this?"

David shrugged. "Army humor." It was either that or admit that he was in deep trouble. "So the front door is out. And I don't think there's a distraction big enough to get rid of those guys."

They checked the view out the front window. Same ugly group.

"I know how you can get out!"

David put his fingertips over her mouth.

Michal pointed to the back of the house and led him through their sleeping quarters. "Remember how I was telling you about the conditions in the alley?" She knocked the wall in a few places.

He frowned. She talked about so many things.

"The ground dips right behind our house and all the waste collects there. Don't you ever smell it?"

"Smells better here than in camp."

Michal rolled her eyes and huffed at him. "Do you at least remember that we used to have a window here?"

"Vaguely." He squinted at the place where she was circling her hand. "Not really."

"Fine." She crossed her arms and plunked herself down on the sleeping mat. "I'm glad our life isn't important to you. I'll be so easy to leave."

David suppressed a sigh. They were in a fight for his life and she was upset that he didn't recall every little thing about the house? He crouched next to her. "Why would I notice a window when you're in the room?"

Her right shoulder lifted and she looked away.

He ran his palm down her long dark hair, lifted the ends to his nose and inhaled. Wildflowers and sunshine. It might be the last beautiful thing he touched and smelled for a long time. If he managed to live a long time. "So there was a window here?"

"Big enough for you to climb through."

"You're a queen among women."

"Of course. Now get to work on that stucco. I'll get a turning fork."

He knocked against the wall where she had, listening for changes in sound. When he was fairly certain he knew the dimensions of the window, he stabbed the center with his dagger and was pleased to see the iron go in a good bit. He hacked a small square and dug it out. By the time Michal returned, he'd hit daylight.

David poked a big chunk through to the outside. It thudded to the ground. "Do you think they heard that?"

She dismissed it with a wave. "They're not going to notice."

"How are you so sure?"

"Our neighbor women are shaking spoons at the soldiers and nagging them about taking over the courtyard." She imitated someone with a high, whiny voice. "I don't care how much trouble David is in, the king is not going to prevent me from providing for my household. As if we'd starve ourselves on the whim of the king. Get your foot off my oven."

As David kept at the painstaking work, a kernel of hope took root in him. Maybe he would get out of this alive.

When it was time for their mid-day meal, Michal

scrounged up some soupy soaked wheat, raisins, dried figs, and a bit of cheese.

"Why don't you go to Eleazar's next door and ask his wife for some fresh bread," David said.

Michal gasped. "With all this, you're complaining about the food?"

"What? No." David tried to smile at her, tried to make it feel like an adventure. "This is a spy mission. While you're there, let her know that I might need a noisy distraction at sleep time."

Her face brightened and she sped down the ladder. He could hear her arguing with the soldiers, using her haughtiest "daughter of the king" voice. Then long silence.

She returned with some bread. "Mission accomplished," she whispered. "Eleazar will meet you behind the watering trough by the gates. He'll bring a rope."

The fresh bread went down his throat in a painful lump. He hadn't wanted to get anyone else involved, but he'd trusted Eleazar with his life for two years in Lachish; he could do it one last time.

They shared a meager meal in the growing rubble of their sleeping quarters.

"Why does my father have to be so afraid of you?"

"I'd never hurt him. Never. " David shifted so he could look into her eyes. "You know that, don't you? I would never do anything to hurt your father."

Michal pressed her lips together and nodded. "That's what makes this so hard."

Too soon, the food was gone and it was back to work. Michal chipped away at the original hole with a turning fork while David made small holes in a square around it.

When the center hole could fit both his hands, he grabbed one edge of stucco, braced his left foot against the wall and yanked hard. It took several tugs, but he managed to pull down a large chunk. Their neighbors were no longer fussing in the courtyard, so he had to carefully place every piece on the floor. By the time they'd opened enough to see over the sky, the sun was two-thirds of the way across it.

David mopped sweat from his forehead and neck. He was blowing on his raw and scratched palms when he heard a thin voice in the distance yelling something about crazy sheep.

The hole was big enough for him to stick his head out. A pack of laughing and yelling children were chasing a knot of sheep down the alley in his direction, making a nice racket. This was his chance to make serious progress.

He grabbed the upper edge of the window with his hands, waited until the commotion was just past the house, and then kicked the bottom edge hard. A good portion fell into the alley. It made enough noise that the little pack turned around, but David smiled and waved and they ran on.

Michal slid to the front room to monitor the soldiers' reactions. David risked it again. When she said that the soldiers hadn't even blinked, he did it a third time and the entire window was open.

Now that air came in from the alley, he could smell what Michal had complained about, but at least he had a way out. He leaned half his body outside: no soldiers to be seen to the right or the left. "What if they're waiting at the end?"

Michal squeezed in next to him and angled her face into the breeze, but then wrinkled her nose and pulled back. "I doubt it. My father told Abner they should watch the front door and arrest you in the morning."

Saul's men were known for their brute strength, not their craftiness, so they would only do exactly what they were told. Unfortunately, Abner was a good strategist. David sighed. He'd have to assume there were more soldiers hidden and ready to nab him.

For Michal's sake, David put on a smile. "Now let's get the rope."

"We don't have one."

"How can we not–" It didn't matter why they didn't have a rope. It wasn't fair to blame Michal for not having what he needed to escape; that wasn't exactly a normal part of household planning. "We'll figure something out." He followed her gaze. "Not your beautiful clothes."

"I can't very well go back out and be seen carrying a

rope home. We don't have to rip them, just braid them together." She leaned out the window. "You can drop a little ways, can't you?"

He wiped as much dust from his hands as he could. "Let's see how long we can get it."

At first, she held the ends and he braided them, but he kept yanking them out of her hands, so they switched.

If she couldn't keep a grip on the rope while he pulled it, how was she going to hold onto it when it carried his entire weight? She wasn't a farm girl, dealing with animals and carrying water every day. She'd always had servants for the heavy lifting.

How else could he anchor the rope?

Would all this work be for nothing?

When Michal finished braiding and went down to get some water, David did a visual check at a side window. Did they have enough to tie the rope to a roof beam and thread it through the room and out the back window?

Not even close. Besides, the soldiers would be able to see him if he did anything at the side of the house.

Michal called for him to help her with the water, so he waited by the ladder. The ladder barely bowed with Michal and the clay jug bumping up it. It was strong.

As soon as Michal was off it, he drew the ladder up and laid it horizontally against the back wall. It fit.

He tied the clothing rope to one of the thick side supports, checked to make sure nobody was in the alley, and threw the rope out the window. It stopped about his height from the ground, long enough that he could hang from the bottom and step down. He drew it back in and gave Michal a loud kiss. “You did good.”

The next task: packing. What to take when he didn’t know how long he’d be gone?

Not his armor. It was heavy and shiny, and the links made too much noise when he walked—not what you wanted in a quiet escape. Besides, he was recognizable in the armor. Jonathan’s cloak wouldn’t be warm on a cold night, but it might come in handy if he had to appear wealthy at some point, so he put it in his pack along with an extra tunic and his regular cloak.

Was it only just before the evening meal that David was training with his men? He was still wearing his battle tunic and it was still tied up so he could move easily. Now he strapped a dagger into his leg sheath and threw three more into his pack, but left his sword with his armor. He’d feel naked outside the city walls without it, but he needed agility more than he needed to be fully armed.

After that, it was a matter of waiting until the sun had dipped below the city walls and it was dark enough that people were heading up to sleep. He’d use the movement of all those feet on their ladders and stairs and scraping across the clay floors and roofs to mask the sound of him scrabbling down the wall.

There was nothing to do but stroke Michal's hair, her beautiful soft hair, and stare out the window.

When they could see only a sliver of sun above the walls, Michal asked, "Where will you go?"

"Somewhere safe."

"Bethlehem?"

"First place they'll go."

"But where?"

The more he thought about it, there was only one place to go. One place where he could finally get his biggest question answered. One place they might not think to look for him.

He choked on the evasion. "A nice big cave until your father forgets about me?"

Michal pleated the hem of his tunic in her fist. "Hebron. I can join you later."

"Can I claim refuge if I haven't done anything wrong?"

"It's better than eating locusts in the wilderness." She smoothed the fabric against his leg. "At least consider it. For me."

He pressed his cheek to the top of her head. "Of course." What else could he say? He knew where he was going, but he didn't want to make her have to lie to her father and he definitely didn't want Saul to be able to get the information out of her.

"Will you send word as soon as you're safe?"

"Of course." Lie number two. This was worse than not

telling his father every time he killed a wild animal to protect the flock. But what choice did he have? "Give my armor and sword to Eleazar. He'll figure out how to get them to me."

"I'll bring them when I meet you in Hebron."

David coughed to relax his throat enough to get the words out. "Give them to Eleazar. Or Jonathan, when he gets back."

The room became dim. They leaned their elbows on the jagged windowsill and watched the sky. Michal pointed out the first star, David the second, and Michal the third.

"Time to light the lamp." Michal's voice was heavy with tears.

After what seemed like endless waiting, all of a sudden, it was time.

David held her close once more, whispered his love and thanks, reminded her that he was hard to kill, and kissed her. And then, while she stomped to the front of the house to light the oil lamps as if everything were normal, he dropped the rope.

Although he could clamber up and down steep, rocky hills like a goat, he'd never had to make his way down a wall like this. He'd seen Philistine soldiers do it *up* their walls. How hard could it be?

His feet couldn't find purchase on the flat wall. Every time his sandals slipped, he was sure the resulting rasp would alert everyone to his escape. But his timing was right; nobody seemed to notice.

He stopped trying to balance on the wall and looped the rope once around his calf and again around his foot, and then put his other foot on top, so he was almost sitting in the air. He could go hand under hand and then slide his legs down. His arms shook with the effort. Michal's clothes were soft and the linen fine, but his palms burned anyway. When his feet ran out of rope, he dropped to the alley. The ladder thudded to the floor in the house.

"Ouch!" Michal yelled. "Stupid lamp." The ladder clattered as if she kicked it.

He held his breath, right hand on his dagger sheath, but there were no yells, no running footsteps from the courtyard.

Michal peered out the window. The moon was low, so she was barely visible. She whispered, "Are you okay?"

"Are you?"

She nodded.

"Me, too." He waved good-bye.

She drew up the braided clothes and he was alone.

20. Escape from Gibeah

David crouched against his house for an hour, waiting for the city to settle down to sleep. The mucky waste that had made Michal plaster over the window seeped over his sandals and squished between his toes. Still, it was better to be standing in filth than in Saul's clutches. He could always clean himself, but he couldn't bring himself back from the dead.

Finally, things were quiet enough that he hitched his pack and headed down the alley, but stopped short after a few steps. There were more stars out and the moon was higher, so it was light enough to see where he was going, which meant it was also light enough for the soldiers to see him in the gap between his house and the next. Even if Saul's men weren't anticipating him escaping out the back, they'd notice movement there–movement they'd have to investigate.

He edged around the corner until he could see the courtyard. The soldiers were all awake. None of them were dozing off. In fact, they were doing an excellent job, watching his front door and his roof, and doing regular visual checks around the courtyard, which meant it was time for some camouflage. He hung his sandals from his belt and smeared his pack and himself with the muck at his feet.

According to every law and custom he was aware of, he was utterly defiled–but with a better chance to avoid detection.

There was movement in the square. This time, when David peeked around the corner, there were twice the amount of men there. They were changing the guard, and not being too quiet about it.

Eleazar's wife poked her head over the parapet next door. "Now?" came her harsh whisper. "Now," David replied in kind.

She crawled to the front of her house and yelled, "Why are you making all that racket? Honest people are trying to sleep."

"We're doing our job," one of the soldiers said.

Another soldier was less kind. "Get back to bed, woman, before you have a bigger problem."

It seemed like every house around the courtyard got into the act. The next time David peered out at the square, all the soldiers were focused on arguing with the people on their roofs. He smiled. A perfect diversion.

He ran in a crouch. Fourteen houses away he could neither see nor hear the commotion in his neighborhood, so he straightened and sped to the watering trough by the gate. He slid in next to Eleazar, who had a length of rope looped around one shoulder.

"Six men," Eleazar reported. "All hiding inside the gate chambers."

David nodded. There was one way out of Gibeah, and Abner made sure they had it covered.

He sat back on his heels and rested his elbows on his knees. There had to be another way to get over the walls.

They were too smooth to climb. If he could get into the fortress, he could go up and over the tower, leap from the roof to the wall and find a way down. There were servants and soldiers in the fortress who were loyal to him, but that was too much of a risk–for them and for him. The king never slept when he was in a rage.

There were stairs and a high ledge on either side of the gate, but that was too close to Abner's guards. One scuffle of his foot and he'd be found out. He might be able to get past one man without raising the alarm, but not six, and not when they had swords and all he had was a handful of daggers. Not to mention the fact that they were brothers in arms; he didn't want to have to hurt anyone.

"But one of those gate guards has a house on the wall," Eleazar said. "With exterior stairs."

"And he's not home to defend it." David didn't dare laugh, but that plan held a certain humor.

Eleazar led the way. They managed to creep up the stairs without waking anyone. David took one end of the rope and drew his guard close. "When my house is clear, take my armor and sword."

"If you get in trouble, head to my mother in Gederah."

David squeezed his shoulder and then hoisted himself up the remaining wall. He waited for Eleazar's, "Go," and then threw the rest of the rope over. He shimmied down, bumping against the wall despite his best efforts to be quiet. When he was halfway down, a woman screamed, "Thief! Thief! He's getting away!"

There was no time to go hand under hand so he slid down the rope, burning his palms and his thighs, and landing in a thudding heap in the dirt.

The rope followed him just after he hit the ground and he sent up a prayer for Eleazar's safety. More people were yelling now, so he tore through the terraced fields and vaulted over low dividing walls.

The south road was the closest, but David circled through the fields until he was headed north. The hills had enough trees that he could move under their cover until he was far enough away that not even the highest scout could spot him.

He set out for the one place he could go, the one place that would give him sanctuary. And, hopefully, answers.

*****

Saul hadn't left the receiving room in four days. But today would be the day. The sun edged over the wall, shining its golden light onto his feet.

He wiggled his toes. Today, he'd finally be freed from David's aggravating goodness, from his military brilliance, from that song that burned in Saul's chest every time he heard it: "Saul has killed his thousands, but David his ten thousands."

His men could appear at the door with David at any time. This time, there would be no dodging, no lucky survival, no negotiated peace. Jonathan was all the way in Naphtali. Even if someone had sent for him yesterday, it would be too late.

Pounding footsteps sounded in the courtyard and he rushed to the doorway. There were his soldiers, but David wasn't with them. Saul drew a blank and then roared, "Where is David?"

"M-m-m-my lord," the group leader said. "Michal said he was sick in bed and couldn't come down."

"She's lying!"

"She said she couldn't come down, either," the man said. "And that the ladder was drawn up so they didn't infect anyone else."

"Look at me," Saul said. "I don't care that she is my daughter. She is standing in the way of what the king wants. Do whatever you need to. Bring him here on his pallet if he can't come out. He's going to be dead soon, anyway."

The soldiers didn't move.

"Now!"

They hustled out and Saul's chest heaved with the effort of keeping himself from running through the streets like a fool and slaughtering David in his bed. Saul's fingers crept to the back of his head and searched for a spot that wasn't too near any of the other still-tender bald spots. He twined a hank of hair around his index and middle fingers and twisted until it came free. Pain flared and faded and he had relief.

He didn't know how long he stood there with the hair in his hand, but he was still there when he heard Michal complaining from the courtyard. He hurried to his throne and shoved the evidence under an animal skin.

Where was his crown? He needed to look more like a king when he dispatched this ultimate judgment on his enemy. He found it across the room where he'd thrown it days ago. The impact of the wall had dented it and knocked off one more ruby, but he put it on his head and clutched the ruby in his right fist. He was sitting tall on his throne before the soldiers entered the room.

Without David. Again.

"Daughter." Saul used his quiet voice. "Where is your husband?"

Michal struggled against the grip of his soldiers. "I don't know."

Saul raised his eyebrows at the group leader.

"We found this idol and a goat's hair pillow in his bed."

Saul's eyes burned in his skull. If they could have shot

fire, his daughter would be a pile of ashes on the floor. It was a pleasing image. "Why have you tricked me and let my enemy escape?"

Michal wailed. "I had to. He threatened to kill me if I didn't let him go."

"My men were right outside your door all day. One sound, one gesture from you and they would've run in and your problem could've been solved."

"He had me by the hair with a knife at my throat, hiding in the back room. What was I supposed to do? He's my husband..."

She kept going, but Saul wasn't listening anymore. Her histrionics were good, but he was enough of a liar that he knew when he was being lied to.

"You must hate him very much," Saul said.

Michal blinked at him.

"Your own husband, the man you loved. How could he betray you like that?"

She shrugged.

"Am I right?"

"As you say." But she no longer sounded convinced.

Saul opened his arms. "Come to your papa. Let me comfort you."

Michal shied away. "This is a matter for women. If your men would let go of me, I'll find Mother."

He stretched his lips into what he hoped was a smile. "No need to be afraid of me. My problem is with your husband, not you. You are my daughter. Come here." He nodded at his men to release her.

She slunk to him.

Once his arms were around her, he whispered, "Your husband is as good as dead. I will find him or someone will give him up."

Michal trembled.

"If you know where he is, tell me now and I won't let his body rot for birds and dogs to pick at."

"You can't get him where he's going."

Saul laughed low and wicked. "I am the king of Israel. No city, not even the cities of refuge–"

Her shoulders twitched.

"So that's where he is," Saul said. "Hebron is the closest one, and it's in Judah, which makes sense."

He put his hands on her shoulders and held her at arm's length. "Thank you, daughter. You know, now that I think about it, you and he were barely together while you were married. It's as if you weren't married at all."

She opened her mouth as if to contradict him so he shook her.

"It's as if you weren't married at all. Which frees you to marry again. A delegation is arriving in a few days to ask for my help on a small matter with Philistia. They'll get some soldiers, but one of them may also get you." He tightened his hands until his fingers dug into her. "Get packed. It's a long, long journey to the territory of Dan."

He shoved her away. "Go! Find your mother and make sure you look like royalty. And don't even think of shaming me."

He wiped his palms against each other, washing his hands of her and her treachery.

His men were still in the room, staring at the ground.

"Get over here. All of you. Now it's your turn." Saul waited until they all stood in front of him. "So, which one of you saw something and second-guessed himself and didn't report it to the others?"

No answer.

"Which of you fell asleep? It's only natural to fall asleep when you're on guard duty all night."

"My lord, none of us fell asleep," the group leader said. "We were alert all night."

"Do not lie for each other." Saul pulled himself to his full height. "I will find out."

They looked resolutely ahead.

"Fine. Then how do you think he escaped right under your very noses?" Despite his efforts to be calm, Saul was yelling by the end of his question.

A man at the end said, "It might have been when the neighbors argued with us."

Saul focused all his attention on him. "Neighbors?"

"When we were changing shifts, some of the neighbors woke up and yelled at us to be quiet, which woke up other neighbors and then people were throwing rotten fruit at us." He hung his head. "We might have been distracted enough for him to escape then."

"You didn't notice him walk out the front door?"

"They busted through the wall in the back and–"

"And none of you heard anything?"

"That would've been the day shift."

Saul took his crown and hit the group leader across the face with it. "Get me the day shift leader and the entire day shift. Bring me the gatekeeper. Search the city. He may still be here. Do it now!"

Abner gave him the news before Saul was served his morning meal. "David didn't get out the gate, but a woman who lives on the wall reported a thief. We found a rope outside the wall, and the wheat is trampled in a line that winds up at the north road."

Saul twisted his beard. "Who can I kill for this fiasco?"

Abner's lips made a thin line.

"David escapes from under our noses and there's nobody to blame?" Saul slapped his palms on the throne. "Don't answer that. Send a delegation of soldiers up the northern road. David could be fooling us and doubling back and heading for his father's house, so send soldiers to Bethlehem, too. I'm not taking any more chances."

Before the end of the day, a messenger reported that David had been spotted in Ramah.

Saul gave the order and then cleared the room.

Ramah. Of course David would run to Ramah.

Samuel was the one who'd said the Lord was giving the crown to someone else, someone better, and now he and that someone better were going to get together and talk about what a terrible king he was. *He* was probably already telling Samuel that David was on his way. David would blush but then fall in line with the plan to make him king. After all, you can't fight *His* will.

Saul pitched his crown at the wall. Again.

It hit next to the spear that still stuck out, taunting him with his repeated failures to get rid of the threat.

He stalked over and wriggled the spear out.

It was such a short journey to Ramah that his men might already be there. They could be back with David before nightfall. Saul fell back onto his throne and wrapped his cloak around himself.

He wasn't leaving this room until it was finished.

21. Too awful and too wonderful

Ramah was just like Bethlehem: no high walls, although individual properties had low walls to keep the livestock in, the dwellings were scattered over the hill, and the well was in the same place on the way into town. David's heart ached from missing his hometown and his legs ached from running full out for an hour.

Now that water was so close, he stumbled until his feet caught up with the rest of his body.

The well was crowded with young girls getting water. They squealed and backed away from him.

He stopped and raised his hands, palms facing them. "Little sisters, I mean you no harm." He dropped to one knee. "I'm nothing but a weary traveler."

The sun glinted off the water in the girls' jars and he lurched forward. They dropped their containers and bolted up to the village.

He scraped his knee as he lunged for one jar before it spilled its contents completely. After he drank everything that was left in it, he looked down at himself. No wonder the girls found him so terrifying. Filth streaked across his body, most of which they could see because his stained battle tunic was still tied high. His thighs were exposed and red from exertion. His hair was matted and dripping. The very image of the villain Saul claimed he was.

He'd better clean up before the village elders arrived. He drew up the bucket at least ten times before the job was done. He poured several bowlfuls over his head even after he was technically clean.

By the time three men approached him, one a lot older and two only a little older than him, he was wearing new clothes and laying out his wet tunic on a rock to dry.

"Stranger, welcome to Ramah," the elder said.

"Good morning, Father. I am David ben Jesse, from Bethlehem." He paused expectantly, but the men kept the same placid looks on their faces. Neither of them said "not *the* David?" or "the giant slayer?" Heat crept up the back of his neck. It wasn't arrogance that made him pause after his name, but experience. Mostly. He cleared his throat. "I mean no harm to Ramah. I come in peace."

That was true, but there was no use in pretending he was merely passing through. "Samuel blessed me when I was a boy. May I see him? Are you able to take me to him?"

"Hold on, now," the elder said. "I am Caleb. My friend Nathan will go to Samuel with your request. Gad and I will wait here with you."

David swallowed his disappointment. "You are wise protectors of your village. I'd expect nothing else."

They sat under the shade of an oak tree and chatted

about ordinary things: the terrible rains of the past spring, how the plantings were looking this year, how the lambing season went. This was the first time in four years that people he met didn't make a big deal about him. It wasn't that he loved the attention, but it felt odd to not get it.

During lulls in the conversation, they peered intently at him, as if expecting him to sprout wings and fly into the sky. There was an odd air of amusement about Caleb and Gad.

Without warning, they stood and invited him to follow them even though Nathan hadn't come back. They strolled through the middle of the village until they reached a low stone wall that set apart a compound on the highest part of the hill.

"This is Naioth," Caleb said. "Where we prophets live."

David blinked. They hadn't told him they were prophets. "Thank you for bringing me here. May the Lord bless you for your kindness."

They laughed, and then waltzed through a wooden gate and gestured for him to follow. He put his hand on the gatepost and looked up at the prophets' compound. David sighed and ran to catch up with the lighthearted men.

Samuel stood alone in a courtyard, looking much like David remembered: short and broad, although his hair was even more unruly now, and all grey and white.

The prophet smiled and opened his arms. "Is that little

forgotten David stuck out in the hills with the flock?" He kissed David's cheek. "Look at you all grown up."

It was fleeting and discreet, but David had been a soldier for too long not to notice Samuel glance at the two men as if asking for a report. They shrugged and left for another building.

"Have you eaten this morning?" Samuel pointed at a mat on the ground. "Sit."

David sat with his back to the house. "What a view." He could see most of the village, the well, and much of the road.

"It's a good spot. I saw you coming, of course." Samuel set out bread, olives, and curds and honey. "Dig in. You look hungry."

He hadn't eaten a proper meal in two days, so he ate until the food was gone.

Samuel chuckled.

"I'm burdening your hospitality," David said. "I apologize."

"Don't be silly." Samuel pointed at his gate with his chin. "You are quite the celebrity."

A dozen or so children had clambered up the wall. David hadn't noticed them because, when his eyes weren't on his food, he watched the road for Saul's men. He gave a little wave and they hid their faces in their hands.

"It isn't every day Israel's great champion comes to our little part of the world."

"Adonai has given me victory."

Samuel patted David's knee. "I'm glad to hear you say so. Excuse me." He wandered down the path and spoke with the children.

David could hear him laughing. When priests came to Gibeah or when David saw them at Gilgal, they were always very serious and ceremonial. Prophets were jolly in comparison.

Samuel returned. "What did you wish to speak with me about?"

"I didn't know where else to go."

"Your father's house is unavailable to you?"

David shook his head. "I haven't done anything to dishonor my father's house. In fact, I haven't done anything to dishonor anyone, yet my return home would put them all in danger."

"Why come here?"

David's gaze darted between the road and the children. "You're right. I should go."

"I said nothing of the sort." Samuel pushed down on his shoulder. "The Lord keeps us safe. Tell me why you're on the run."

"How did you know I was on the run?"

"You ran up the road half-naked and just told me you

can't go to your father's house because it would put them in danger."

David squeezed his temples and rubbed his eyes. "It's King Saul. I haven't done anything against the king, I swear it, but he wants me dead. I barely escaped last night."

"That makes sense."

"It does?"

"Come now, think about it." Samuel stacked their bowls. "Adonai has left Saul and is with you. You're a threat to him."

It was amazing that Samuel could make such a pronouncement while doing housekeeping. "I am not."

"You are not actively threatening him, no, but your very existence puts his kingship in jeopardy and he knows it."

David frowned. "How?"

Samuel smiled. "Honest men are usually the last to figure these things out."

The prophet was silent for so long that, out of desperation, David blurted his real question. "Why did you anoint me?"

"Why do you think?"

"Was it to defeat the giant, Goliath?"

"What do you think?"

"I thought so at the time."

"But now?"

David's heart thudded. "Saul is Adonai's Anointed."

Samuel whispered, "But not the only one."

David shook his head vehemently.

"Did you learn to hear His voice?"

"Yes." Don't ask, don't ask, don't ask, don't–

"What does He say to you?"

Samuel's tone was matter-of-fact, as if Adonai speaking to a person was a normal occurrence, but David couldn't form the words.

"You are supposed to be the most courageous man of your generation. I suppose those reports are exaggerated."

"It is you," David mumbled.

"Speak up." Some of the good humor left Samuel's voice.

"'It is you.' That's what He tells me. But I don't know *what* is me."

"Yes, you do. Your humility is edging over into stupidity. What do you think He's been preparing you for?"

It was hard to speak through the lump in his throat. "It's too awful and too wonderful at the same time."

Samuel gave a great bark of laughter. "You have the gist of Adonai exactly. No wonder He calls you a man after His own heart."

David startled and swallowed wrong and struggled through a coughing fit. A man after His own heart? He was a scared twenty-year-old on the run for his life.

Samuel patted David's knee. "Rest now. Talk with

Adonai about what I've said and let Him speak to you. Give Him time to do so. The Lord is patient, but young men, not so much."

They sat together in the sun of the courtyard while other prophets came and went, while women baked bread in the ovens and boiled wheat over small fires, while children ran back from gathering firewood, nobody paying them any attention, as if it were the usual thing for two grown men to sit and do nothing.

At first, David squeezed his eyes shut and pleaded with Adonai to tell him whether he truly was meant to be king, but even asking that question flooded him with guilt. Saul was grooming Jonathan to be king. How could he snatch the throne from his best friend?

Eventually, the sun and lack of sleep and stress of the escape caught up with him, and he found his head nodding. He tried to force his eyes open, but it was a losing battle.

The next thing he knew, his chin was on his chest and Samuel was shaking his shoulder. "Go inside and get some real sleep."

David muttered something he intended to sound like, "If you're sure," but even he couldn't understand what came out of his mouth. However, something he saw on the road when he stood woke him instantly: Saul's men.

They found him so quickly. Too quickly. He wasn't ready to leave Samuel, not after the boulder the prophet dropped in his lap. But he couldn't fight off a dozen of the king's men in this state.

David shouldered his pack. "I wish we had more time."

"What?" Samuel squinted at the road. "Oh, you mean them. Go inside and rest." He indicated Saul's men with his thumb. "They won't get anywhere near you."

"I don't want anyone to get hurt on my account."

"Don't worry about us. We have an impregnable defense."

David didn't want to offend the prophet, but he looked around pointedly. There were no walls and nobody was sounding an alarm or preparing for armed conflict.

Caleb approached Samuel, grinning. "I take it these guests coming up the road are ones the Lord will take care of?"

"But they're His people." David couldn't believe they could be so glib about the death of their countrymen.

Samuel took on the look of a teacher. "Adonai doesn't need to kill to accomplish His purposes. Sometimes, the best recourse is to give Himself more fully and completely than those people ever had or will have again. Their current course will become impossible and they will be filled with shame." He put his arm around David. "Truly, it's worse than if the Lord struck them down on the spot."

"The Lord hasn't let anyone with evil intent get close

to the gates of Naioth in years," Caleb said. "They usually don't get past the well, do they, Samuel?"

The two prophets laughed as if remembering good old times. David didn't understand what they were talking about or what was so funny, but he knew Adonai could do unexplainable things.

"It's hotter than Sheol on my roof," Samuel said, "but you can cover yourself and hide up there to watch the Lord move. Caleb, let's go help those soldiers see the folly of their ways."

David crouched with his cloak over his head and peered over the parapet, watching Samuel and Caleb stride to the well, gathering others along the way. There were fourteen of them by the time they reached Ramah's outskirts. As the soldiers got closer, all the prophets did was stand arm-in-arm in a circle and sing. Snatches of melody made their way back to him and raised the hair on his forearms.

The squad leader gave the signal and the soldiers unsheathed their weapons and spread out in formation. The bronze and iron glinted like lightning, but the prophets didn't acknowledge them in any way. When Saul's men were mere steps away, the prophets broke apart and formed a line, but it was like no defensive line David knew of. Some of them stood with their arms raised to the heavens, others fell on the ground, pounding the earth with their fists, and still others whirled in wild circles, the hems of their tunics flashing above their knees.

David watched, slack-jawed, as, one by one, the soldiers dropped their weapons and joined the men of God in their worship. Tears fell unchecked as he watched these rough soldiers be overcome by the Spirit of Adonai.

And then he laughed—not because the soldiers looked foolish, but out of utter security in the Lord's protection.

The soldiers shrugged out of their armor; some threw it up in the trees. The commander lay on his back, spread-eagled. Another man stripped down to his loincloth and whipped his tunic up and down and back and forth in a frenzy. There was no defending against Adonai. Praise rolled off them like a wave.

David had relied on the Lord to save him before, but this was different. It wasn't Adonai plus his own skill or Adonai plus his own strength. There was no other response than to revel in His presence.

He threw off his cloak, stood with arms wide and his palms up, tilted back his head, and sang like he hadn't sung in too long.

> Adonai is my strength.
> He shields me from every danger.
> I trust in Him with all my heart.
> He helps me, and my heart fills with joy.
> I burst out in songs of thanksgiving.

The soldiers and prophets were still at the well, still consumed by the Spirit of the Lord. David's heart beat hard and his blood charged through his body, but his limbs and his head were heavy, and growing heavier. He didn't need to watch anymore. He trusted Adonai to let him wake up in safety.

No wonder those prophets laughed so much.

*****

Saul glowered at the fourteen men he'd sent after David yesterday. He waited to speak until their fear came at him like a heat wave. "You're lucky the gate guard warned me you were coming without the one I charged you to bring to me."

He huffed several loud breaths through his nose. "Somebody better start telling me what happened, including what in the name of the stars and the sun happened to your weapons and your armor?"

"It's hard to explain." The squad leader's skin turned redder than the ground in the Negev.

"Try."

"We got to Ramah and there were prophets by the well."

These were not the brightest soldiers in his army, but surely they could report on what happened yesterday. Saul cleared his throat. "And then."

"It's hard to..."

"Spit it out!"

The leader closed his eyes, took a deep breath, and spoke in a rush. "They were worshipping and prophesying and before we knew it, we'd thrown our weapons down and joined them. The next thing any of us knew, it was morning and our weapons and armor were melted into a lump in the middle of the remains of a fire and someone had left food for us. We ate and came back here."

Saul studied the ceiling. He couldn't look at them anymore. "Was David there?"

"We–we didn't see him, but we heard him singing."

"And you didn't go get him?"

"The Lord wouldn't let us."

Him. It all came back to *Him.* Saul breathed steadily to push down the rising tide of nausea. "Get out of my sight." He lunged at them. "Go! Go back to your fathers. Go back to Ramah for all I care. You're all dead to me. Go before you're all dead for real."

He buried his fists in his hair, grabbing as much as he could as close to his scalp as he could and held it tight until the chaos inside him ebbed. "Abner! Abner! Someone fetch me Abner!"

"I'm right here, my lord."

Saul pointed out the door. "Those men. Those men were fools and idiot sheep. David is at Ramah but they didn't even make it past the well. Get me fourteen more—no, get me twenty-one more men. Warn them that Samuel is there and he'll try to trick them by making them pray with him. Stuff flax in their ears, deafen them for real, tell them to sing dirty songs right back at the prophets. I don't care how they do it, but they will bring David back."

"My lord, I'll do whatever you ask," Abner said. "But I beg you to eat something."

Saul saw the pile of bowls and cups by his throne. He hadn't realized anyone was bringing him food.

"You need your strength."

"Are you saying that I won't have what it takes to get rid of my enemy when I'm faced with him?"

Abner sighed. "Cousin, just eat."

Saul picked up a piece of bread. It was hard as a rock. He picked up another that was still pliable and tore off a bite. It was his favorite, fried in oil and drizzled with honey, but it tasted like nothing. Still, he swallowed it. Abner was right. Tiresome, but right. He needed his strength.

The next morning, it was the same thing: his twenty-one soldiers returned with their weapons in a knot, as meek as downy lambs, with a story about prophets and being overcome by *His* Spirit.

Saul sent out twenty-eight men.

The morning after that, the outcome was identical. No matter how tough the men, no matter that he threatened them with cutting off their beards and sending them back to their fathers with their tunics cut up to their navels, the result was the same.

There was only one solution. He had to send someone who was immune to *Him*. Someone *He* hated. Saul had to go himself.

22. Someday

Saul would get to David *and* make sure Samuel knew that he couldn't keep toying with Saul's kingship. Saul was king. *He* and Samuel made it so, and Saul had won battle after battle after battle to earn the right to remain so and to give the crown to one of his sons.

He removed his gold armlets and his linen garments and put on clothes from one of his armor bearers: a rough wool tunic and a cloak with no tassels and no embroidery, and a plain cloth to wind around his head, everything a dull shade of brown.

It took a small portion of the morning to travel to Ramah, but his clothes were soaked by the time he arrived. In this heat, it was probably sun sickness that had afflicted his soldiers.

He'd taken seven soldiers with him, but once he spotted the well at the base of the village he made them hang back. Whatever happened between him and Samuel, he didn't want anyone close enough to hear the exchange.

There was nobody at the well when he got there, so he raised the jug himself. He was pouring water over his face when he heard the crunch of footsteps.

"Greetings, stranger. What a day for travel."

"Ramah is blessed to have such a sweet and abundant

well." Saul barely remembered to bow his head at the man. Here, he was a stranger hoping for some hospitality and information, not the king.

"The Lord has blessed us richly, indeed. What brings you on the road on a day like this?"

"I am from the clan of Aphiah in Benjamin. I seek an audience with Samuel."

"Is that all you seek?"

Saul shrugged. "Just relief from curiosity. I've heard from some men on the road that a singer of heavenly skill has recently come to Ramah. Tell me, is the one they call David still here?"

The man raised his chin and blinked slowly. "David is still here." He turned and pointed at the highest point in the village. "He's in Naioth with Samuel."

"Naioth?"

"The prophets' compound. Would you like me to take you there?"

"I'd be grateful." Could it be this easy?

Saul had barely gone ten steps when dots of white light showed up in his vision. He rubbed at his eyes, but they got thicker. Soon, all he could see was light, no forms, no colors, no shapes, just whiteness. He called out to the stranger but couldn't understand the response. And then it was like thunder rumbled toward him, except there was no sound. Vibrations rose from the earth and up his bones to the top of his head until he found himself face-down in the dust.

Image after image sliced through him, coming almost too fast to understand: the fields of his father's household, being anointed in secret, being anointed at Mizpah, being anointed at Gilgal. Battles flashed by. And then his sins, oh his sins, one after the other after the other.

He writhed on the ground.

"The Lord will save you, Saul." That was Samuel's voice. "Release yourself to His mercy."

Saul screamed like a bird.

"You remember how." Samuel's voice was low and gentle, like it was when he first anointed Saul. "Let Him in."

Saul's back arched like a bow. He couldn't let go. *He* would incinerate him.

"Call Him by name," Samuel whispered. "You remember what it was like, how sweet it was."

Remembering wasn't the problem. It was what happened after the letting go. It wasn't fair of the Lord to desert him for all those years and now to swamp him, to overcome him, to entice him.

Tears and sweat and snot streamed down and mixed with the dust. He breathed in the grit and ground it between his teeth.

"Even after everything." Samuel was so close that the prophet's breath warmed Saul's ear. "Adonai loves you."

Saul had no defenses strong enough to resist that.

Nobody loved him. They feared him, or respected him, or derided him.

The Lord loved him.

Any barriers between him and this love were offensive, so he threw off his clothes and returned to the ground. He could vaguely hear people around him saying things, but he didn't care. For one of the few times in his life, he didn't care what people thought. This love, the love of the Lord for him, filled him until he must be shining as bright as a star.

Over and over, he whispered it: Adonai. Adonai. Adonai.

*****

David crept closer but kept his distance. He couldn't believe what he saw. "Is Saul a prophet, too?"

Samuel shamed him with a glance.

"Are you sure it isn't a trap?"

"With how hard he fought?" Samuel shook his head. "You're safe. He'll be like this until morning."

They watched Saul praise the Lord and prophesy. His eyes were open, but he didn't seem to see anything around him.

David knelt beside him. "He's usually so bitter against the Lord."

"How do you know that?"

"He'd talk while I played for him. Most of the time, I don't think he knew I was listening."

"But you were?"

David nodded.

"Consider that part of your education," Samuel said. "As were these last few days here with me, as were your years in the army."

"And my time as a shepherd?"

"Don't sound so skeptical. People are about as smart as sheep and you know how to lead sheep."

David shifted.

Samuel put his hand on David's shoulder to hold him there. "Let's stay with the sheep. Whose sheep were they? Yours?"

"No. They were my father's."

"Were any of them yours?"

David shook his head.

"Not even after you'd been their shepherd for a long time and they knew and trusted your voice?"

"No." David snorted. "I wouldn't get any even if my father died. They'd all go to my older brother."

Samuel squeezed David's shoulder. Each word was as heavy as a sack of grain. "The people are the Lord's and you will be their shepherd."

"I like to call Adonai *my* shepherd."

"So then you are His under-shepherd."

David gazed down at Saul. Was that part of the king's

problem? Did he forget that? David wiped his palms on his tunic and stood.

"You look different than when you came to us."

"True. I'm not covered in filth."

"Not that." Samuel steered David away from Saul. "You carry yourself in a new way now that you can't deny what the Lord wants of you."

What was he supposed to say to that?

Samuel's heavy hand landed on the top of his head and he prayed.

David couldn't understand a word the prophet said, but he closed his eyes and let the heat and power radiating from Samuel's hand travel through his body.

Samuel released him and stepped back. "There will be difficult years ahead. Saul won't give up his throne easily."

David scuffed his sandal on a rock. "I won't have to kill Saul or Jonathan, will I?"

"Why do you ask?"

"Because I won't. I won't harm Adonai's Anointed or gain the throne by murder. I love Jonathan like a brother, more than any of my actual brothers. And don't look at me like I'm a cute kid with high ideals that won't survive into adulthood. I'm–"

"That's not what I was doing." Samuel's voice was gentle, but it was enough to stop David's rant. "Did I ever tell you about the time I became Israel's judge?"

David shook his head.

"I'd been a prophet since I was a boy, but Eli had died and we kept losing against the Philistines. I kept after the people about getting rid of their idols and returning to the Lord. Finally, they wanted to repent. I led them to Mizpah. We fasted and prayed and confessed our sins and poured out great bucketfuls of water before the Lord. It was beautiful."

The last few days had taught David that Samuel told stories like his Uncle Jonathan's: long, but reaching a point eventually. He settled in to listen.

"In the middle of all this, someone ran up from Gibeon to tell us the Philistines were on their way." Samuel leaned forward. "I mean, there we were, all of Israel's powerful as well as hundreds of the not-so-powerful, gathered in one place. They were terrified, weeping, shouting, and, in general, carrying on as if we were already in a funeral procession."

He shook his head. "Anyway, they clamored for me to plead with the Lord on their behalf, so I did. I sacrificed a lamb as a whole burnt offering, which takes some time. They had to find a lamb. I had to build a fire, kill the lamb, sprinkle the blood on the altar, cut it into pieces, and then wash the head and internal fat. I made them all wait with me, no running off to fight. If they wanted to hear from the Lord, they were going to hear from the Lord."

Samuel chuckled. "They were straining like the lamb did when I had its neck under my arm, but I kept praying and doing what I had to do. They were whipping their heads around, looking behind them at the Philistines, and then back to me, and then back to the Philistines. I swear we could see the whites of their eyes. Finally, it was time to put the lamb on the altar. The fire sputtered for a second and the people gasped, thinking that the Lord wasn't going to accept their sacrifice and we were all doomed, but then the flames whooshed around the animal and shot high. At the same time, the Lord's voice thundered down. The Philistines were so terrified and confused that it was a simple matter for us to turn around and chase them all the way to Beth-car."

David narrowed his eyes. "So all that is to say that the Lord will make it happen in His own timing and in His own way?"

Samuel winked.

"Now let me tell you a story," David said, and the prophet cupped his hand around his ear. "My oldest brother knows he'll get my father's household some day. He's always known it. So he acts like he's already the head, ordering the rest of us around, using his fists and his feet to lord over us. And we can't say anything against him, because he will be our head of household some day. But if he were to leave Bethlehem to join another village, none of us would go with him. None. I will not, *not* be like him."

The old prophet nodded. "Someone new, someone better, indeed." But there was no time for David to ask what he meant by that, because he rushed on. "I normally say to people, 'May the Lord be with you,' but I know He'll be with you. Instead I'll say, 'May you always turn to Adonai.'"

David's breath shuddered. "So this is real?"

"Very real."

"Can I come back for counsel?"

Samuel snorted. "You don't need me to speak with the Lord on your behalf or to hear from Him. You've been doing both for years."

"So this is it?"

"For you and me, yes." Samuel pulled him close and kissed both cheeks and his forehead. "This," he gestured to Saul on the ground, "won't last, so everything you do from now on must not only keep you safe from Saul, but must also go toward preparing yourself and the people for your kingdom."

Responsibility settled on David's shoulders like a heavy mantle. What could he say to Samuel that covered everything he felt?

Samuel playfully shoved David. "I hate long good-byes."

David laughed with him and set off down the road with a wave. He slowed and put his right hand on the dagger at his back when he saw the men Saul must have brought with him.

They circled each other on opposite sides of the road.

"Have you killed him, then?"

"I will never, never–" David's voice got thick and he

stopped to bring it under control. "*Never* kill Saul. But you should go to him. He'll need you soon enough."

David set out with no men, no family, no armor, no sword, and no home to go to. All he had was Adonai and the promise that he would be king of Israel.

Someday.

*****

Look for the next installment of the story, *The Noble Outlaw*, which follows David for the next ten years as he's on the run from Saul, trying to survive and figuring out how to shepherd the men who flock to him in the wilderness, forming a pack of outlaws 600-strong that he never asked to lead. He'll be forced to lie to the high priest, join the mercenary force of the king of Gath, and avoid getting killed by King Saul and the thousands of soldiers who are after him–all while trying to figure out how and when Adonai will make him king when he refuses to kill Saul.

To follow the progress of *The Noble Outlaw*, sign up for the mailing list at http://writtendeer.com.

Glossary

Adonai – the name for God in Hebrew

anointing – the act of pouring oil on someone's head or rubbing their head with oil so as to confer divine honor or blessing upon the anointed one

ben – "son of," so David ben Jesse is David son of Jesse

cloak – outer garment, not necessarily a coat as we think of it, but may just be a single piece of fabric draped around a person and fastened at the neck (like a cape) or held in place by a belt and/or a mantle

lyre – portable stringed instrument

mantle – decorative clothing item with fringe, often worn over the shoulder; an indicator of the high status of the wearer

ox goad – long stick with a pointed end, used to prod oxen into action

pagan – non-Israelite; one who doesn't believe in the Lord as the only god

prophet – person who listens to God and speaks His words to the people

Shema – prayer that is part of daily Jewish life as well as prayer services

Sheol – the pit; a place where the dead go, deep in the earth *sling* – square of leather with two leads, one attached to each side; one lead ends in a loop to be put around a finger, the other ends in a knot; the slinger nestles a stone in the square, holds onto the knot end of the leads, and rotates the stone quickly (often side-arm) and releases the knot to launch the stone forwards

threshing floor – an open space either inside or just outside of a village where people take their harvested grains to separate the usable parts from the chaff; often a village meeting place

tunic –the basic item of clothing; either a rectangle of cloth folded in half and sewed up the sides with two holes left open for arms and a hole cut in the top for the head, or two rectangles sewn together; it may be knee-length for working in the fields or longer for more ceremonial situations

wadi – stream; many streams are seasonal and are full in the winter and spring, but drier (sometimes completely dry) in the summer

yoke – wooden bar that goes across a person's or a pack animal's shoulders to help them carry heavy burdens

Bible Verse List

In writing this work of fiction based on biblical stories, Hart slightly altered many Bible verses, mostly from 1 Samuel and the Psalms. Here is a list of verses that are more or less directly quoted, in the order in which they appear. All verses are from the New Living Translation unless indicated otherwise.

Chapter 1 – Psalm 8:5

Chapter 2 – Psalm 24:1; Psalm 21:13; Psalm 20:7; Psalm 29:2

Chapter 4 – Psalm 19:5-6

Chapter 7 – Psalm 105:1-2, 5, 8-11, 41-42; Psalm 13:1-3; Psalm 19:7-8, 10; Deuteronomy 6:4 (NIV)

Chapter 8 – Psalm 68:1-2, 11

Chapter 9 – Psalm 33:16-17, 20

Chapters 10/11 – Scattered verses from 1 Samuel 17; Psalm 59:10

Chapter 12 – 1 Samuel 18:7; Psalm 21:1; 1 Samuel 15:28

Chapter 14 – Deuteronomy 6:4-5; Psalm 18:25

Chapter 15 – Psalm 118:15; Psalm 68:4

Chapter 17 – Psalm 8:3-5

Chapter 18 – Psalm 124:2-5; Psalm 59:17

Chapter 21 – Psalm 28:7

Discussion Guide

For additional resources on the culture and geography of ancient Israel, see http://writtendeer.com/biblical-research and https://www.pinterest.com/writtendeer/the-giant-slayer. Hart also posts about ancient Israelite culture, geography, botany, etc., on Facebook https://www.facebook.com/nahartauthor.

Chapters 1-3

1. What is David's relationship like with his father? With his brothers? With his Uncle Jonathan?
2. What do you think is important to Jesse? To Uncle Jonathan? How can you see this in their interactions with David?
3. What is daily life like in 1000 BCE for an average family?
4. How would you describe David to a friend? Do you like him? Do you relate to him?
5. Experts in ancient Israelite culture say that Saul wasn't a king like we think of a king, with a fancy castle and well-established cultural traditions: the first king of Israel was more like a really powerful tribal chief. What are some examples of this in the

opening chapters?

6. How would you describe King Saul to a friend? Do you like him? Do you relate to him?
7. How would you describe Jonathan to a friend? Do you like him? Do you relate to him?
8. The name for God that Samuel and David use is *Adonai.* That is how people would read the name for God in Hebrew, which was written YHWH. At the end of Chapter 2, Saul does, too. How does Saul feel about God when he calls God "*Him*"? How does he feel about God when he calls God "Adonai"?

Chapters 4-6

1. One of the reasons Hart wrote this book was to help readers experience the story as David and Saul went through it at the time. It's easy to think that David was a high-status servant because *we* know he'll eventually be king–but nobody knew that at the time. According to *The Giant Slayer*, what was David's life like as a servant of King Saul?
2. You won't find the first song David sings to Saul in Chapter 4 anywhere in the Bible. Even the story in 1 Samuel 10:9-13 about Saul acting like a prophet isn't like this. Hart read an intriguing book that posited that, after David was king, his scribes changed a story about Saul's cunning and bravery into one that

made him appear foolish. This will come to fruition in the third book of the series, *The Shepherd King*. What do you think of the idea that Saul might have been more impressive than we think he was?

3. How was the Israelite army gathered? How did they train? How did they get supplies? Did soldiers join the army as a year-round profession?
4. What is David's relationship with his father like now? With his mother? His siblings?
5. How would you describe Joab to a friend? Do you like him? Can you relate to him?
6. In Chapter 6, David is concerned about his cleanliness. This is only a little bit about whether he's physically dirty. Cleanliness in the Old Testament is also about holiness. Leviticus 11-15 details the many things that can make a person unclean. The solution is usually to wash the body and the clothes and stay away from people until evening, with some uncleanliness requiring washing in water that is moving. We saw this in Chapter 1, when Eliab makes David wash in a fresh spring instead of with well water. Do you think Eliab makes David wash in running water because he's concerned about David's holiness? Or do you think he was being mean? Do you think everyone took those cultural expectations as seriously as David did? What does that tell you about David's character? What does that tell you about

how people live out rules in general? Think about the people you know: Do you all always follow rules perfectly? Why or why not?

Chapters 7-9

1. In Chapter 7, we get Saul's anointing story (you can also find it in 1 Samuel 9-10). How is Saul's anointing story similar to David's? How is it different?
2. Do you feel like you understand Saul a little better? Do you have sympathy for him? How would you feel if you were chosen for something you never wanted, succeeded at it, but were always being negatively judged? List all the emotions Saul experiences in this section. How would you describe Saul's relationship with God?
3. What does David learn in this section about his father? About Saul?
4. David is sixteen by this point in the story. How has he matured since he was twelve? How is he still the same?
5. What are the practical things David has to deal with for his trip to the battlefront? Can you think of other ways he could've dealt with them?
6. What do you think Uncle Jonathan means when he says, "War is more and less than you could ever imagine"?

7. What does David notice at the battlefront that tells him this isn't a regular battle?
8. What are the emotional highs David goes through in this section? What are some emotional lows?

Chapters 10-12

1. How is David both right and wrong in his analysis of how the army is reacting to Goliath?
2. Describe David's relationship with the brothers he interacts with in this section.
3. How did David's mind change from trying to get the other soldiers to fight the giant, to offering to fight the giant?
4. Why do you think Saul wanted David to wear his own armor? Was it out of a desire to protect David? Was it out of a desire to be seen as the one taking action? Something else?
5. In a TED talk, https://www.ted.com/talks/malcolm_gladwell_the_unheard_story_of_david_and_goliath, Malcolm Gladwell claims that David's simple technology and skill as a slinger made him well equipped to win against Goliath, even though nobody else recognized that at the time. How were David's disadvantages turned into advantages? Who does David credit?

6. If you read 1 Samuel 16:14-23 and 17:55-18:4, you will notice that there are two different accounts for how David meets Saul. Hart tried to account for that by having Saul almost always close his eyes while David is playing for him, and by treating David as a servant (not as a special guest). Did it work? Did you believe that Saul could see David on the battlefield and not immediately know who he was?
7. What was David's first battle like after he joined in the general fighting? Compare it to when he'd played with Joab back home.
8. What is Saul like in battle? Is he different than he is in his receiving room? How or how not?
9. Describe Saul's mood and how it changes during the long march back home. How do you think you would feel if you were in his situation?
10. The story Saul tells David is from 1 Samuel 15. Read it and answer this: Can you understand Saul's point of view? Can you relate to him? Have you ever tried to justify your actions even though you knew they were wrong? If you got called on it, how did that make you feel?

Chapters 13-15

1. Do you believe the excuse Saul gave to himself and to Jonathan about why he threw his spear?
2. Was David crazy for remaining in Saul's service? Or did he have good reasons to stay? Or are both things true? If David were your friend coming to you for advice, what would you tell him?
3. Why do you think David wanted to hide the giant's sword on the way to the sacrifice?
4. Why do you think David was upset that Eliab wanted to use David's fame to get them food? Do you think he should have been upset?
5. The descriptions of the priests was taken from Exodus 28, and the rules for the sacrifices from Leviticus 1 and 3. Some groups still do mass sacrifices at festivals; look up "Samaritan Passover sacrifice on Mount Gezirim." Does the portrayal in *The Giant Slayer* seem plausible? Did anything surprise you about it?
6. Does anything change between David and his father in this section? Explain.
7. Why do you think Saul made David a military leader? What do you think of how David handled the situation? What do you think of David's speech to his men in the morning? Would you have joined his unit?

Chapters 16-19

1. What do you think was Saul's *real* reason for making David a military leader?
2. How would you describe the relationship between Saul and Jonathan?
3. How would you describe Saul's family life?
4. What is David's relationship like with his men?
5. Why do you think David dragged his heels so much about marrying one of Saul's daughters? Why did he eventually give in?
6. In Saul's time, they said he was tormented by an evil spirit. How would you describe what Saul's problem is? What are the coping methods he's used throughout the book? Are they all successful?
7. Is Jonathan a good judge of the problem between Saul and David? Is he a good mediator? Do you have faith in the peace he negotiated?
8. How does David and Jonathan's relationship change (in both good and tough ways) in this section?
9. What do you think of David's decision to go to Saul in Chapter Nineteen? Did he have a choice?
10. Did David and Michal work well together in the escape?

Chapters 20-22

1. How did David escape the city without being detected?
2. What do you think of how Saul treated Michal? How do you think his treatment made Michal feel?
3. What did you think of the portrayal of the prophets as being so light-hearted? Why might a prophet be different with people than a priest?
4. Why do you think it was so difficult for David to admit what God was asking of him?
5. What do you think of these words of Samuel: "Sometimes, the best recourse is to give Himself more fully and completely than those people ever had or will have again. Their current course will become impossible and they will be filled with shame later....Truly, it's worse than if the Lord struck them down, dead on the spot." How would you describe what happened to Saul and his men?
6. Why do you think David refuses to kill Saul? Is it for the reasons he tells Samuel? Or might there be other reasons?
7. What is the purpose of the story he tells Samuel about Eliab?
8. Does Samuel and David's final conversation give you any hints about what kind of king David will be?

Wrapping it up

1. What are some ways David's time is different from your time? What are some ways it's the same?
2. How do they tell time in 1,000 BCE? What markers do they use to signal the passage of time?
3. How do they measure physical objects?
4. Reflect on who used the name *Adonai* for God. Did you feel like the people who used it had a different kind of relationship with God than the people who didn't use it?
5. Who do you relate to more, David or Saul? Or someone else in the story?
6. What do you think are the main differences between David and Saul?

Acknowledgments

Although writing is an often solitary endeavor, publishing definitely is not. I say a hearty *thank you* to all these fine people who contributed in some way. To my beta reading crew: Will Van Houten, David Van Dyke, Kees van Liere, Thomas van Liere, Isaac Lundell, Anya Dengerink-Van Til, and Ben Swedberg. To my developmental editors, Lindsay Tweedle, Helen Hart, and Sharon Van Houten–particularly to the last two, who read the manuscript multiple times. To my adult beta readers: Sara deBoer, Dawn Elliott, and Karl Westerhof.

To the ministers whose sermons delivered key insights into David: Dr. Robert L. Stevenson, Jr. and Rev. Jack Kooreman. To my Old Testament expert, Rev. Sarah Schreiber. To Mary Loebig Giles for her marketing writing and indie publishing wisdom.

Thank you to those who have encouraged my writing: my book club friends, my Renew and Refine friends, my Writer Unboxed UnCon friends, my Grace Church family. Special thanks to the Hart and Van Houten clans for your support over many, many, many years. To Michael Van Houten for pushing me out the door to writing conferences when I was terrified to do so. To Willem Hart and Ben Van Houten for the beautiful graphic design work that I didn't wind up being able to use—thank you, and please forgive me.

A huge thank you to my parents: to Peter Hart for his entrepreneurial spirit and example, and to Helen Hart for her steadiness and for enabling my love of reading since the beginning. To Richard Mulligan for the love and joy he brought back to my life, thereby refueling my writing. To Christina Van Dyke for her deep and sustaining friendship. And to my children, Will and Hannah, who are the only people I nag—bringing this novel to life has forced me to practice what I nag about, and I am so grateful for their love and their laughter along the way.

And I'd like to thank God for all the things he's taught me through this writing and publishing process, chief of which is that I have done what he's asked of me just by writing. But the most lasting thing I have taken to heart during the long slog of indie publishing this novel that I began in 2012, is that I am God's beloved. I am his beloved whether I write a word or not. I am his beloved even if I do nothing. I think David had that knowledge, too, and managed to hang onto it his whole life, whereas it kept slipping through Saul's fingers. Here's hoping I'm more like David in that respect.

About the author

N.A. Hart grew up in Toronto, Canada and Brisbane, Australia, and lived in three of the five boroughs of New York City, but wound up in Grand Rapids, Michigan. Family and cheap real estate drove her to it. She has been telling Bible stories to kids and teenagers for over twenty years. The Old Testament is her favorite because it's full of real people who are mixed bags of failure and faithfulness, fear and trust–just like she is. She has two adult children. Her online home is at nataliehart.com, but she's also on Facebook at www.facebook.com/nahartauthor and barely on Twitter @NatalieAHart.

CPSIA information can be obtained
at www.ICGtesting.com
Printed in the USA
FSHW012158260319
56700FS